Lorraine Hansberry's

The Sign in Sidney Brustein's Window

A DRAMA IN TWO ACTS

REVISED STAGE EDITION

SAMUEL FRENCH, INC.
45 West 25th Street NEW YORK 10010
7623 Sunset Boulevard HOLLYWOOD 90046
LONDON *TORONTO*

Printed in U.S.A.

ISBN 0 573 61541 1

NOTE TO THE PRODUCER

PROGRAM NOTES AND PRESS MATERIALS:
Any of the introductory and supplemental materials in this edition may be reprinted in your playbill or distributed to the press as background to the play.

Plays by Lorraine Hansberry
available from Samuel French

A RAISIN IN THE SUN
(25th Anniversary Revised Edition)

LES BLANCS (*THE WHITES*)

RAISIN (The Musical)

THE SIGN IN SIDNEY BRUSTEIN'S WINDOW
(Revised Stage Edition)

TO BE YOUNG, GIFTED AND BLACK

For
Robert Nemiroff
and
Burt D'Lugoff
and
the committed everywhere

CONTENTS

A NOTE ABOUT THIS REVISED EDITION

When the original production of *The Sign in Sidney Brustein's Window* opened in 1964, Lorraine Hansberry was in the midst of a real-life drama of her own that transcended anything on stage: the battle against the remorseless cancer which finally claimed her life three months later. In the critical period of the play's staging, it was thus impossible for her, except very sporadically, to attend rehearsals to put the finishing touches on the work which had occupied her, on and off, for four years. Hansberry was able to see the entire play on its feet only a few nights before the opening and, overall, was gratified by what she saw. But she did feel the need for tightening, for some small but important clarifications of relationships and themes, some shifts in dramatic pacing, and (in one area) a restructuring to sharpen the focus on Sidney and Iris. She did some telling rewrites at that time—too late, alas, to go into performance until after the opening—and she discussed with me others that she planned. But she could not complete the final honing she felt the play needed to achieve its full potential.

The present script addresses that task. It is the fruit of those last discussions with Lorraine Hansberry about the play and of my own observations—as producer of the original and as the playwright's literary executor—of many productions over the years; and of, in some instances invaluable, discussions with the principals in some of these (I am particularly grateful to the late great director Alan Schneider for his insights and help in this regard). In completing it, I went back, too, to the playwright's original working drafts to draw upon those lines and approaches that might prove most cogent in effectuating the result she sought.

The culmination of this process came with a showcase production by New York's Richard Allen Center, where it was possible to try out and put ideas to the test. The result was unmistakable: the response of the audience overwhelming, the reviews unqualified. Significantly, these emphasized not just the power of individual scenes, the humanity and strength of the characters, as had always been the case,* but the *unity* of the play and the contemporaneity of the playwright's vision.

Still I needed to be sure. I offered the revised script to other local productions and some outside New York. The results were the same.

The present revision, then, incorporates into the play cuts, clarifications and some restructuring, with material by Lorraine Hansberry from earlier drafts and some additions of my own.

In sum, my own additions are too small to call it an adaptation. This is Lorraine Hansberry's play—in form, finally, I believe, to achieve its full impact and the recognition it has always deserved.

Robert Nemiroff

HANSBERRY ARCHIVES: For the Lorraine Hansberry Archives, we would be grateful to receive programs, reviews, pressclips, etc., and any pertinent comments concerning productions of the Hansberry plays. Please address these to Robert Nemiroff, c/o Samuel French, 45 West 25th Street, New York, NY 10011.

*For a sampling of reviews through the years, see back cover and pp. 140–143.

THE SIGN IN SIDNEY BRUSTEIN'S WINDOW was first presented by Burt C. D'Lugoff, Robert Nemiroff and J. I. Jahre at the Longacre Theatre, New York City, N.Y., on October 15, 1964, with the following:

CAST OF CHARACTERS*

(in order of their appearance)

SIDNEY BRUSTEIN .... Gabriel Dell
ALTON SCALES .... Ben Aliza
IRIS PARODUS BRUSTEIN .... Rita Moreno
WALLY O'HARA .... Frank Schofield
MAX .... Dolph Sweet
MAVIS PARODUS BRYSON .... Alice Ghostley
DAVID RAGIN .... John Alderman
GLORIA PARODUS .... Cynthia O'Neal

Directed by Peter Kass
Scenery by Jack Blackman
Lighting by Jules Fisher
Costumes by Fred Voelpel
"The Wally O'Hara Campaign Song" *by* Ernie Sheldon
Production Associate: Alan Heyman
Associate to the Producers: Beverly Landau

SYNOPSIS OF SCENES

The action of the play takes place in the Brustein apartment and adjoining courtyard in Greenwich Village, New York City, in the early 1960's.

ACT ONE

SCENE ONE: Early Evening. The late spring.
SCENE TWO: Dusk. The following week.

ACT TWO

SCENE ONE: Just before daybreak, next day.
SCENE TWO: Evening. Late summer.
SCENE THREE: Primary Night. Early September.
SCENE FOUR: Several hours later.
SCENE FIVE: Early next morning.

---

*The original production also included the walk-on role of a detective, played by Josip Elic, which has been eliminated.

PRODUCTION NOTES: THE SETTING

The setting is Greenwich Village, New York City—the preferred habitat of many who fancy revolt, or, at least, detachment from the social order that surrounds us.

At the rear are all the recognizable sight symbols of the great city. They are, however, in the murk of distance and dominated by a proscenium foreground which is made up of jutting façades. These are the representative bits and pieces of architecture which seem almost inevitably to set the character of those communities where the arts and bohemia try to reside in isolation—before the fact of their presence tends to attract those others who wish to be *in* bohemia if not *of* it—and whose presence, in turn, paradoxically tends to drive the rents beyond the reach of the former. Tenements of commonplace and unglamorized misery huddle together with cherished relics of the beginning days of a civilization: the priceless and the unworthy leaning indiscriminately together in both arty pretentiousness and genuine picturesque assertiveness.

Thus, here is a renovation of a "Dutch farmhouse"; there, a stable reputed to have housed some early governor's horses; and here the baroque chambers of some famed and eccentric actor. And leading off, one or two narrow and twisty little streets with squared-off panes of glass that do, in midwinter, with their frosty corners, actually succeed in reminding of Dickensian London. The studio apartment of the Brusteins, at Left, is the ground floor of a converted brownstone, which—like a few other brownstones in the Village—has an old-fashioned, wrought-iron outside staircase arching over a tiny patio where city-type vegetation miraculously and doggedly grows. Beneath the staircase landing is the Brusteins' private entrance. Nearby, Downstage Right, is a tree.

In the cut-away interior of the apartment the walls are painted, after the current fashion in this district, the starkest white. To arrest the eye—because those who live here think much of such things—the colors which have been set against it are soft yellows and warm browns and, strikingly, touches of orange, vivid sharp orange, and that lovely blue associated with Navajo culture. We can see at once that the people who live here would not, even if they did have a great deal of money—which they certainly do not—spend it on expensive furnishings. They prefer by pocket book and taste—to the point of snobbery perhaps—to scrounge about the Salvation Army bargain outlets; almost *never* the "Early American" shops which are largely if not entirely priced for the tourist trade. In any case, a few years ago most things would have been discernibly "do-it-yourself" modern in these rooms, but that mood is past now and there is not a single sling chair or low, sharply angled table. "Country things" have come with all their knocked-about air and utilitarian comfort. But there remain, still, crafted ceramic pots of massive rhododendrons in various corners and, everywhere, stacks of last year's magazines and a goodly number of newspapers. The result is that —while it is not a dirty place—*clutter* amounts almost to a motif. Prints range through reproductions of both the most obscure and the most celebrated art of human history, and these, without exception, are superbly and fittingly framed. And there is a sole expensive item: a well-arranged hi-fidelity unit, and, therefore, whole walls of long-playing records, and not one of them at an angle. Fighting them for supremacy of the walls, however, are hundreds and hundreds of books. And on one wall—Sidney's banjo.*

In fine, it is to the eye and spirit an attractive place. Its carelessness does not make it less so. And, indeed, one might lounge here more easily than in some other contemporary rooms—and, perhaps, *think* more easily. Upstage Center is the bedroom door. To its Right, the bathroom. Downstage Left is part of the kitchen area, which disappears Offstage. Downstage of the whole apartment is the street through which characters may enter from right or left. And, dominating all, Upstage Left, the large irregularly shaped bay window, angled out from the building wall in a skylight effect, in which will presently hang—the *Sign in Sidney Brustein's Window.*

---

*Or some other appropriate instrument if the actor happens to play one.

The Sign in Sidney Brustein's Window

ACT ONE

SCENE 1

TIME: *The early Sixties. An early evening in late spring.*
PLACE: *Greenwich Village.*
AT RISE: *SIDNEY BRUSTEIN and ALTON SCALES enter arguing* D.L. *and cross to the apartment door, each burdened down with armloads, two or three each, of those wire racks of glasses that are found in restaurants. They have carried them several blocks and are out of breath as they struggle with the loads.*

SIDNEY is in his late thirties and inclined to no category of dress whatsoever—that is to say, unlike his associates, who tend to the toggle-coated, woven, mustardy, corduroy appearance of the post-war generation of intellectuals in Europe and America. This has escaped SIDNEY: he wears white dress shirts as often as not, usually for some reason or other open at the cuffs—but not rolled; old college shoes; and whichever pair of trousers he has happened to put on with whichever jacket he has happened to reach for that morning. It is not an affectation; he does not care. He is, in the truest sense of the word, an intellectual: his passion is ideas, words, language. If he cannot control *his world, at least he can* articulate *it—which, more often than not means to* mock *it. He is not a pedant, but a man who questions ev-*

erything—and has a great deal of fun about it—yet retains the capacity for wonder and a free-wheeling lust for life. An idealist and, more than a little, a clown—who laughs at himself as much as the world. He does not *wear glasses.*

ALTON is a youth of 27, lithe, dark, with close-cropped hair and the mustardy, corduroy and sweatered look of the Village. He is, to the eye of the audience, white, *but his manner and speech are rich with the colorings and inflections of black idiom.*

SIDNEY. . . . It's your story, man, but Jesus Christ— (*attempting to balance the glasses and find his keys*) it's not about Imperialism and the Ghetto!

ALTON. The hell you say. Any time a black kid—

SIDNEY. And it's not about his mother either. (*fumbling with key and lock*) Damn. (*He opens the door and deposits his load in the middle of the living room floor. ALTON kicks door shut behind them and racks his glasses on top of SIDNEY's.*) Never mind the kid's mother, for Christ's sake! And never mind the tears in his sister's eyes. (*as ALTON straightens to face him*) Look, even if it *is* Willie Johnson—if you're gonna write for *my* newspaper, Alton, write it like you figure we already *care* without you sending up organ music. Follow?

ALTON. (*stiffly*) I hear what you are saying.

SIDNEY. But compassion is *consuming* your heart and you want us to *know* it, right?

ALTON. He may die. The doctors said—

SIDNEY. And you think I don't know that? You think I'm not *there* right with him? But *this*— (*pulling a half-dozen typed pages out of his pocket*) is not going to save him! Look, baby, from now on: (*indicating himself*) new publisher—new policy! When you write for the *new*

Village Crier, let's forget we absolutely *love* mankind. Don't venerate, don't celebrate, don't—

ALTON. Don't cogitate, don't agitate—

SIDNEY. (*nodding*) Our readers don't want it. That's why Harvey had to unload the paper.

ALTON. You're gonna wear out your ass sitting on that fence, man.

SIDNEY. And above all else: keep your conscience to yourself. It's the only form of compassion left. (*hands ALTON the story; lights a cigarette and wanders back to the glasses which he suddenly confronts; with mock funereal gravity, making the sign of the cross over the racks*) So there they are: the last remains of Walden Pond.

ALTON. You're better off—what the hell did you know about running a nightclub, man?

SIDNEY. (*old refrain*) It wasn't a *nightclub*.

ALTON. You can say that again. Not with a name like Walden Pond. And it wasn't a restaurant or a coffee house or anything else that anybody ever heard of.

SIDNEY. I thought there'd be an audience for it. A place just to listen to good folk records. For people like me. There gotta be people like me somewhere.

ALTON. There are. And *they* don't go to nightclubs to listen to records either.

SIDNEY. It wasn't *supposed*—

ALTON. (*cutting in*) ". . . to be a nightclub." I know. (*dryly*) "Walden Pond."

SIDNEY. Well, whatever it was, let's drink to it. (*picks out two glasses*)

ALTON. Bourbon for me.

SIDNEY. (*lifting out one of several bottles in the racks*) You can have vodka *with* ice or vodka *without* ice. (*Pours; they toast and drink.*) Let's get to work. (*Hauls out huge pad and marking crayon and sits at drawing board, which is framed by the window; it is angled almost horizontally to serve as his desk.*)

ALTON. (*idle curiosity—that is not so idle*) Ahh—Sid . . . Does Iris know you've *bought*—and I use the term loosely—the paper yet?

SIDNEY. (*laying out the first page with broad strokes*) Not yet.

ALTON. Well, don't you think she oughta know? I mean, like, a wife—

SIDNEY. Yes, I'll tell her.

ALTON. When? It's been two weeks already.

SIDNEY. (*trapped, therefore evasively*) When I get a chance, I'll tell her.

ALTON. She's going to have a lot of opinions about it.

SIDNEY. She always has opinions. You know what? I think I'd like to try our first issue in reverse. White print, black paper. What's with this black on white jazz all the time? People get in ruts.

(*IRIS enters* D.R. *with armful of groceries and crosses to door. Not yet thirty, she is quick with a gamin vivacity that utterly charms, and possesses vast quantities of long dark hair, done up in a French twist. Whatever her talent on stage, IRIS* is *an actress, given to playful mimicry and overdramatization which, at least with SIDNEY, she plays to the hilt. Between them, though this is not their actual age relationship, there is more than a little of the adolescent girl showing off for father, seeking his approval, testing the limits of his knowledge and authority. He has been her lover, mentor, universe, god. But, increasingly of late, there has been the insistent, though as yet unidentified need to break free. This tension between them bubbles freely to the surface; yet, save in their sharpest exchanges, still in a context of loving banter and fun. At the CLICK of the lock, SIDNEY thrusts pad aside. She enters, sees the glasses but says nothing as she crosses to deposit groceries on bar, pecks ALTON, and crosses back—her eyes never once having left the racks. SIDNEY kisses her cheek.*)

IRIS. (*firmly*) I don't want them in my living room. (*crosses away*)

SIDNEY. Where else can I put them?

IRIS. We're not going to have the residue of all your failures in the living room. (*takes off raincoat to reveal yellow-and-white counter waitress uniform*)

SIDNEY. Look. Don't start. It's over, isn't that enough?

IRIS. It was over before it started, if you ask me. (*putting up groceries*)

SIDNEY. It would have done okay if that publicity creep had done a better job on the publicity.

IRIS. He thought he should be paid.

SIDNEY. I offered him a piece of the place!

IRIS. Who wants a piece of a non-profit nightclub?

SIDNEY. *It wasn't a nightclub!*

IRIS. Believe me I know.

SIDNEY. (*as ALTON edges toward the door*) Alton, I thought you were—

ALTON. (*sweetly*) I just remembered a very pressing engagement someplace.

SIDNEY. ("Don't desert me.") Where?

ALTON. I'll think of it later. (*exits* U.R.)

(*SIDNEY puts a RECORD on and IRIS slips out of dress into tights and bra. The MUSIC comes up. It is a white blues out of the Southland,* "Babe I'm Gonna Leave You": *a lyrical lament whose melody probably started somewhere in the British Isles centuries ago and has crossed the ocean to be touched by the throb of black folk blues and then, finally, by the soul of back-country crackers. It is, in a word, old, haunting, American, and infinitely beautiful, and, mingled with the voice of Joan Baez, it is a statement which does not allow embarrassment for its soaring and curiously ascendant melancholy. SIDNEY beckons and IRIS crosses into his arms. They kiss, embrace playfully, then sink onto the couch. He reaches for the pins in her hair.*)

SIDNEY. Take down your hair for me, Mountain Girl.

IRIS. (*She breaks away, laughing.*) Sidney, I just got home . . . (*Replaces the pins; she does a few warm-up dance* plies. *SIDNEY watches, then imitates. She does* plie *and extends an arm. He follows suit. She does so again, but this time whacks his stomach. He desists, she continues. Then, too casually:*) Ben Asch was in for lunch.

SIDNEY. (*sobers as it registers; finds his way to drawing board*) So?

IRIS. He said they're doing a tent production of *South Pacific* out on the island. Casting now. And guess who's doing it? (*He says nothing, deliberately busying himself at the board.*) Harry Maxton! (*no response*) Sidney, *Harry Maxton!* Remember, he *loved* me when I read for him that time? (*She crosses to shut off RECORD, drops to knees and sings with the fixed "Oriental" smile and hand gestures of the original. He sobers and looks away.*)

"Happy talk, keep talkin' happy talk
Talk about things you like to do.
If you don't have a dream . . ."

(*The gestures continue as the voice trails off.*) Remember? He really flipped for my Liat!

SIDNEY. (*automatically, not looking at her*) And he hired somebody else. And you know perfectly well you won't show up for the audition. (*He is immediately sorry.*)

IRIS. (*frozen in the "Liat" pose*) You rotten, cruel, sadistic, self-satisfying son of a bitch! (*crosses away to begin another set of dance exercises*)

SIDNEY. I'm sorry. I don't know why I do that.

IRIS. (*exercising*) Then why don't you *find out* and give us both a break!

SIDNEY. Does Dr. Steiner really tell you to go around drumming up business for him like that?

IRIS. (*flauntingly, with superiority*) I have *not* mentioned Dr. Steiner! And I am *not* going to. I am not *ever* going to mention Dr. Steiner in this house again. *Or* my analysis. You don't understand it. You can't—

SIDNEY and IRIS. (*together, he wearily with her*) —"unless you've been through it yourself!"

SIDNEY. (*As she reacts, he mimics her singing.*)

"Happy talk, keep talkin' happy talk . . ."

IRIS. Well, that happens to be true! (*back to exercises*)

SIDNEY. Iris, honey, you've been in analysis for two years and the only difference is that *before* you used to *cry* all the time. And now you *scream.* (*a beat*) Before you cry. (*Having scored he crosses to bar and mixes drink.*)

IRIS. YOU DON'T GET BETTER OVERNIGHT, SIDNEY, BUT IT IS HELPING ME! Do you think I would have been able to say the things I just said if I wasn't going through a TREMENDOUS change?

SIDNEY. (*genuinely curious*) What things?

IRIS. I just called you a sadistic, self-satisfying son of a bitch to your face—instead of just *thinking* it. (*He looks at her blankly.*) Well, don't you remember when I couldn't say things like that? Just *feel* them—but not *say* them?

SIDNEY. Which amounts to you paying that quack half your paycheck to teach you how to swear. Lots of luck! (*In frustration she picks up rack of glasses and deposits it on his lap.*)

IRIS. It's *my* paycheck. And that's not the point!

SIDNEY. I'm sorry. Swear *out loud.*

IRIS. (*through her teeth*) For someone who thinks that they are the great intellect of all times, the top-heaviest son of a bitch that ever lived—

SIDNEY. (*cupping his hands like a megaphone*) Another step toward mental health!

IRIS. (*moving closer and leaning in to him*) For someone who thinks they've got the most *open* mind that was ever opened, *you* are the most narrow-minded, provincial—

SIDNEY. —"insular and parochial—"

IRIS. —insular and parochial bastard alive! (*crossing behind him coyly*) And I'll tell you this: I may be whacked up, sweetie, but I really would hate to see the inside of your stomach. (*"loving" pat of his stomach*) Oh-ho, I really would! St. John of the Twelve Agonies, I'll tell you.

SIDNEY. (*quietly amused*) I am *not* agonized.

IRIS. *Everyone* is agonized!

SIDNEY. Iris, how do you know this?

IRIS. (*with great superiority*) *Everyone* knows it. *Der*—(*hesitates and mispronounces the word*) *Ang-oost* is Everywhere.

SIDNEY. (*slow take; oversweetly*) *Ahhngst.* A-N-G-S-T. It means anguish.

IRIS. (*glaring at him*) And I'll tell you this, if I had all your hostilities—

SIDNEY. Look, Iris, three years ago you practically tore up our marriage looking for a sex problem, because one fine day you decided we *had* to have one—because "*everybody* has one." We even *invented* one for six months to keep Steiner happy. Well, I promise you, this time we are not going to embark on the search for my—*Angst*!

IRIS. (*lying flat on back and raising one leg, then the other; darkly teasing*) I happen to know some things about you *in bed* that you don't know.

SIDNEY. (*dropping to his haunches to peer at her*) Then tell me about them so we can discuss them.

IRIS. (*an air of the holy*) *Oh no!* No sirree. Get thyself to a professional. You're not going to catch *me* engaging in parlor analysis!

SIDNEY. There was nothing to analyze. It was merely a little matter of technique. (*huskily sexy*) There are just some things in bed I like— (*embracing her*) —and some I like MORE!

IRIS. (*in the sway of his arms—playfully*) That just shows you: nothing about *sex* is *just* technical. And I notice I'm not the one around here with an ulcer. And I must say that for a contented man, who just *happens* to have an ulcer, you drink one hell of a lot.

SIDNEY. (*sitting up; sore spot*) It's *my* ulcer!

IRIS. (*back to exercises*) Basically, Sidney, you are an ambivalent personality. You can't admit to disorder of any sort because that symbolizes weakness to you, and you can't admit to health either because you associate that with superficiality—

SIDNEY. Iris, please, shut the hell up, I can't stand it when you're on this jag! (*He reaches for her again: this precious foolishness is all a game he loves.*)

IRIS. (*shouting*) Then why didn't you marry somebody you could talk to then! (*It hangs a second, is ab-*

sorbed with minor melancholy by SIDNEY who, to rise above it, offers a parodied Elizabethan flourish.)

SIDNEY. Because— (*lifting his drink like Cyrano*) "What did please the morning's academic ear did seem indeed— (*bringing the hand down defeatedly*) to repel the evening's sensuous touch. Think this poor poet not cruel to say it, but— (*concluding with a flourish*) gentle Sid, be but a mortal thing."

IRIS. (*feminine cruelty*) Awwww, is that what you told poor Evie when she proposed?

SIDNEY. She didn't propose. Cut it out.

IRIS. You said she did.

SIDNEY. Bedroom boasts. You don't pretend to believe mine and I won't pretend to believe yours. (*turns her face to him gently*) What you were supposed to say was: "In such regard and diluted esteem doth my master hold his own sweet Iris—"

IRIS. I don't know the piece. What is it?

SIDNEY. (*dully, staring off*) Nothing.

IRIS. What?

SIDNEY. Plutarch or some damn body!

IRIS. Well, whatever it's from, it said you really do think I'm stupid!

SIDNEY. It said: I love you. It said I do not counsel reason or quarrel with my nature. It said, girl, that I love my wife. Curious thing. (*stops her lips with a kiss*)

IRIS. Meaning frivolous mind and all.

SIDNEY. You make a silly fishwife. Stop it.

IRIS. Can't I say *anything*?

SIDNEY. Not in this mood, it's driving me crazy! (*He gets up agitatedly and goes to the window and looks out at the street.*)

IRIS. (*resolute anger*) And one thing is clear: You prefer picking at me to talking to me. (*She crosses into the bathroom to brush her teeth with door open. On the inside of door are a towel rack and mirror. Sink and medicine cabinet are visible inside.*)

SIDNEY. (*shouting*) I do not! And tell that Dr. Steiner to take his love-hate obsession and— (*restraining himself*) Look, let's talk about how we are going to get you to that audition.

IRIS. (*brush in hand*) Sidney, why can't you understand about the blocks that people have?

SIDNEY. I do understand about them and I know that if they are nurtured enough they get bigger and bigger and—

IRIS. (*glaring at him*) All right, Sidney. All right. (*She finishes in bathroom and marches out.*) So I haven't worked out my life so good. Have you? Or are those glasses I see before me a MIRAGE!

SIDNEY. No, Iris, they are not a mirage. Look, nobody's perfect. I may have made a few slight miscalculations, but . . . (*throws up his hands*) Aw, what do you know about it?

IRIS. (*undulating away with triumph*) I know there is no great wisdom in opening a folksong nightclub where there are something like twenty such in a radius four blocks square. I know that, darling-pie!

SIDNEY. (*painfully: old refrain, lost cause*) It wasn't *supposed* to be a nightclub—

IRIS. Don't remind me. (*crosses into bedroom and returns with sweater and tight high-water pants which she pulls on as they talk*) And what are you going to do with all those glasses?

SIDNEY. How do I know right now? There have to be places that need 150 sturdy restaurant glasses, don't there? I'll take care of it.

IRIS. You know when they *audit* the place they're going to think it's awfully funny that they're no glasses. I mean, a night— (*smiles*) —*spot* with no customers, maybe . . . but no *glasses*!? What're you going to say happened to them?

SIDNEY. How should I know what happened to them? Maybe somebody broke in and stole 'em. Why should I know every little detail?

IRIS. (*giggling*) Auditors *love* details, Sid. They specialize in details.

SIDNEY. I said I'll take care of it! You oughta be grateful I had the foresight to at least salvage something out of it *before* they audit! (*Tickles her to change the subject; she escapes.*)

IRIS. Right. I'm grateful. "Foresight." (*She turns back the cover of SIDNEY's pad to reveal the layout on which he had been working; picking it up.*) So now what? You're going to be an artist? This is *aw-ful*. (*a fit of appropriate giggling*)

SIDNEY. It's not supposed to be a drawing. It's the layout for the new— (*He halts, not having meant to get into this this way.*)

IRIS. (*already expecting almost anything*) For the *what*, Sidney? For the "new" *what*?

SIDNEY. (*He exhales heavily.*) Harvey Wyatt met this chick—

IRIS. Yes, *and*—?

SIDNEY. —he decided to go live in Majorca, forget the whole scene and just like that go live in Majorca . . . I mean you know Harvey, he's a great—

IRIS. Yes, *and*—

SIDNEY. (*shrugging*) So he *had* to unload the paper.

IRIS. Oh my God, no. Oh, please, God, don't let it be true. Unload it on—*whom*? Oh, Sidney, you haven't . . . ?

SIDNEY. I know it's hard for you, Iris, to understand what I'm all about—

IRIS. (*slumping where she is*) I don't believe this. I don't believe you could come out of—of *that*— (*gesturing to the glasses and then to the pad*) and get into *this*! Aside from anything else, what did you conceivably tell Harvey you were going to pay him?

SIDNEY. We made an arrangement. Don't worry about it.

IRIS. I'm not worried about it what kind of arrangement, Sidney? (*no pause between the two sentences*)

SIDNEY. An arrangement. I know what I arranged.

IRIS. Where in the world are you going to get the money to pay for a newspaper?

SIDNEY. It's a *small* newspaper. A weekly.

IRIS. Sidney, you can't afford a *yearly leaflet*!

SIDNEY. Look, this is a real rich babe Harvey's hooked up with. He's not worried about the money.

IRIS. Good.

SIDNEY. Just yet.

IRIS. When? (*a beat*) And when he *is*, Sidney?

SIDNEY. Why isn't it ever enough for me to tell you that I know what I'm doing? I'll raise it, that's all. I raised it for Walden Pond! I'll raise it for the *Village Crier*. In order to *do* things you have to *do* things!

(*During the above WALLY O'HARA, a conventionally dressed man in his early forties, and ALTON have approached,* D.R. *WALLY carries several cardboard placards. For a moment the two stand in conversation. Now ALTON beats on the door. IRIS throws up her hands, dons sweater, and admits them.*)

ALTON. (*kissing her broadly; gesturing toward WALLY*) Hey, look who I ran into.

WALLY. (*Shows poster to SID and IRIS. It reads:* "O'HARA FOR REFORM.") Hey, Sid.

SIDNEY. (*standing stock-still, resolutely*) The answer is no.

ALTON. Don't be a clown! At least hear what the man has to say!

SIDNEY. I know what he has to say and I don't want to hear it.

(*Despite the seriousness and passion of the discussion that follows, the tone is effervescent. These are old friends, buddies carrying on as they always have: clowning, slashing, parrying, mugging, mocking with alacrity.*)

WALLY. Iris. (*He kisses her.*) How's life in the pancake world?

IRIS. Don't ask. (*She goes into the kitchen, hands ALTON knife, bowl, and vegetables to cut up, and busies herself in kitchen.*)

WALLY. Sid—

SIDNEY. Wally, my little artsy-craftsy newspaper is going to stay out of politics. *Any* kind of politics. Period.

WALLY. (*abruptly dropping the posters like typhoid-carriers*) Yes, I know. "Politics are dirty, fetid, compromise-ridden exercises in futility." Etcetera, etcetera, etcet— (*noting the glasses and picking one up*) A bunch of big drinkers here? (*pours himself a drink*) Nonetheless, Sidney, I've finally faced up and it's time you did too: there is work to be done. Now I'm risking a budding law practice—

SIDNEY. Look, Wally, I love you madly, but—

WALLY. Sidney, just listen please. For the sake of all those all-night raps at Walden Pond, okay? (*SIDNEY is quiet.*) Even if we don't win at least we can lay a helluva groundwork for next time. Now my neck is on the chopping block in this primary and all I'm asking is a little legwork and the endorsement of what—I take it—is now your paper.

SIDNEY. Sorry, Wally. Not even for you. The *Crier* endorses no one. My readers can do as they please.

ALTON. (*to WALLY*) There it is, man! The great disease of the modern bourgeois intellectual: (*burying his head*) *ostrich*-ism! The great sad withdrawal— (*plunges knife into stomach and expires*) from the affairs of men.

SIDNEY. (*turning in kind on ALTON*) Yes, Alton, I admit it: I *have* lost the pretensions of the campus revolutionary. I no longer have the energy, the purity or the comprehension to—"save the world." As a matter of fact, to get *real* big about it, I no longer even believe— (*inverting Shelley's classic affirmation:* "If Winter comes can Spring be far behind?") that "Spring" must necessarily come at all. Or that, if it does, it will bring forth anything more poetic or insurgent than— (*with a flourish*) the winter's dormant ulcers.

WALLY. We're not talking about the world, we're talking about this community. It's like they tell you in A.A.: Don't think about all the drinks you've got to give up, just concentrate on the next one. That's the trick, Sid. Don't think about the ailing world for once, just your own little ailing neighborhood. (*pins up a poster*)

SIDNEY. That's very impressive. (*takes poster down and hands it back*) But the truth of the matter is, dear friends, that I have experienced the *death* of the exclamation point! I no longer want to exhort anybody about anything. It's the final end of boyhood.

ALTON. And the beginning of senility!

SIDNEY. Of course, some people— (*looking at ALTON*) are just one *long* exclamation point!

ALTON. (*sauntering over into his face*) Yeah? Well, like, no matter how you punctuate it, capitulation has one smell, one shape, one sound—

SIDNEY. And insurgency one speech! Look, baby, I'll match your credentials any day! You wanna see my scrapbooks? Since I was eighteen I've belonged to every committee to Save, to Free, to Abolish, Preserve, Reserve and Conserve that ever was. And the result— (*playing it to the hilt*) is that the mere thought of a "movement" to do *anything* chills my bones! I simply can no longer bear the spectacle of power-driven insurgents trying at all cost to gain control of— (*The coup de grâce: deflated balloon.*) the refreshment committee! (*He crosses into bathroom for his bottle of pills.*)

WALLY. (*smiling easily*) I told you: think only of not taking the next drink.

SIDNEY. You mean diddle around with the *little* things since we can't do anything about the *big* ones? Forget about the Holocaust and worry about—reforms in the traffic court or something? (*takes his pills with a drink*)

WALLY. (*putting his down with vigor*) Christ, man, this is the second largest narcotics drop in the city! The syndicate acts like it owns this neighborhood. The Real Estate Board runs a bigger game, the cops get theirs like clockwork, the politicians keep the lid on, and smack in the middle sits the machine—

SIDNEY. Wally, I told you—

WALLY. (*riding over him*) —while kids like—what's his name, the busboy who worked at Waldon Pond—?

ALTON. Willie Johnson.

WALLY. Kids like Willie O.D. on shit! (*a beat*) I tell you, Sid, if my corniness offends you, sorry. But I'd like to see the Willie Johnsons have a real chance in this city.

SIDNEY. (*dismissal*) Wally, I wish you luck, I'll even vote for you, but leave me out of it. Iris, beer!

IRIS. (*opening refrigerator*) All I've got to say, Sidney, is just *mean* what you say for once in your life, just *mean* what you say.

WALLY. (*strictly in jest*) All of which goes to prove that a woman's place is in the oven. (*IRIS jabs him playfully as she hands him his beer.*)

ALTON. (*mugging*) With the door closed!

(*The PHONE, on wall* L. *near counter, rings.*)

IRIS. Jesus, that'll be Mavis. I don't feel like Mavis tonight. Sid, you get it.

SIDNEY. I never feel like Mavis. You get it. (*IRIS does. To ALTON soberly:*) Speaking of Iris's sisters, I hear you've been seeing a lot of Gloria.

IRIS. (*on phone, throws a swift warning glance at her husband*) Sid-nee—

ALTON. (*mugging heavily and smacking lips*) Yeaa-ahhhh. (*to WALLY*) You should *see* this one, man! (*waving his fingers for the heat*)

WALLY. I'd like to—

IRIS. (*cutting in, one hand cupping the receiver*) —Can't. She's in Los Angeles.

ALTON. Gloria travels a lot. High-fashion model, you know. (*He passes a photo of GLORIA to WALLY and SIDNEY.*)

IRIS. (*on phone*) I am listening, love. I don't care, Mav—I don't want it, that's all. Goodbye! (*hangs up* *with a final Greek expletive*) *Asto diabolo!** She's got another dress for me—

SIDNEY. Dear old Mavis, Mother of the Philistines . . .

IRIS. Quit putting her down all the time, Sid. Just cut it out, okay?

SIDNEY. (*utterly confused*) But you always do—

IRIS. She's *my* sister! (*He suddenly pulls the pins out of her hair, causing it to fall down all over her.*) Oh, damn it, Sid! Don't start with the hair bit, I told you! (*Putting her hair up, she disappears into bedroom with a string of Greek expletives.*) *Asi meh vray vlaka, ta kokoria na seh faneh!***

ALTON. What's the matter with her lately?

SIDNEY. Who knows? Maybe she's changing life.

WALLY. Come on, it's the Greek in her. You should know that. The triumph of the innate tragedy in her soul.

SIDNEY. (*for IRIS to hear*) She's only half Greek, so she should only be half tragic. Hey, Iris, when you come back out, turn up just one side of your face.

IRIS. (o.s.) Boy, are you fellows fun-nee! (*a wild cackle of sardonic laughter*)

WALLY. Hey, what *is* the other half?

SIDNEY. Irish 'n' Cherokee. I am married to— (*circus barker*) the only living Oklahoma Greco-Gaelic-Indian hillbilly in captivity. If one can think of Iris as being in captivity . . . Do your dance, honey. (*Her arm snakes sexily out of the doorway, then her leg. Then, as SIDNEY and ALTON clap and sing along, she snakes out dancing and chanting the Greek Miserlou—which turns into a jig, and then into a stereotypical "Indian" war*

---

* Pronounced: Ah-stoh' dee-ah' boh-loh.

** Pronounced: Ass' ih meh vray vlah' kah, dhah koh-koh' ree-ah nah seh fah' neh.

dance, to conclude with a Marilyn Monroe freeze—and an abrupt "Up yours!" finger to SIDNEY.) I taught her everything she knows! You should hear my mother on Iris. "Not that I have anything against the *goyim*, Sidney . . ."

IRIS. (*picking it up*) "What can I say, Sidney, she's a lovely girl. But, Sidney, she's no *balabusta* . . ."

SIDNEY. "Lambfat?! *Schmaltz* from a *lamb*?? *Oi vey!* . . ."

IRIS and SIDNEY. *"Like a lump on the stomach it sits!"*

IRIS. (*to WALLY and ALTON*) Ha! She should only know her *son*! If he had *his* way, he'd have me running barefoot through the woods in a gingham dress.

SIDNEY. And I'd be running bare-assed after you! (*He sweeps her up in his arms.*) Hey, what d'ya say we give *all* our clothes to Mavis, pack a couple of sandwiches, some records, my books, and take off—

ALL. (*in unison*) —up to the mountains!

SIDNEY. (*painfully*) Yes. And stay . . . (*looking into her eyes*) Forever. (*She sighs and he puts her down.*)

ALTON. (*who has been flipping the pages of a book on the coffee table*) You know, your trouble, Sid, is that you admire the wrong parts of Thoreau.

SIDNEY. Oh, How do you know what parts—

ALTON. You mark passages. (*starts to read aloud, facetiously trilling his r's*) ". . . In the bare fields and tinkling woods see what virtue survives . . . A cold and searching wind drives away all contagion, and nothing can withstand it but what has virtue in it . . ."

SIDNEY. (*plucking the book out of his hands to read with sober feeling*) You read rotten. "Whatever we meet in cold and bleak places, as the tops of mountains, we respect for a sort of sturdy innocence . . . It is invigorating to breathe the cleansèd air . . . and we fain would stay out long and late, that the gales may sigh through us, too, as through the lifeless trees, and fit us through the winter: — as if we hoped so to borrow some pure and steadfast virtue which will stead us in all seasons." (*SIDNEY closes the book thoughtfully and a little defiantly.*)

WALLY. (*applauding lightly*) Beautiful. Beautiful. But how's about the rest of Thoreau, Nature Boy? Poor old Henry tried his damnedest to stay in the woods, but the world wouldn't let him — it never does. What about that, Sidney? What about the Thoreau who came *back* and called the first public meeting to defend John Brown? What about the Thoreau who was locked up in jail when that holy of holies, Ralph Waldo Emerson, came strolling by and asked: (*playing it*) "Well, Henry, what are you doing in there?" And Thoreau, who was "in there" for protesting slavery and the Mexican War, looked out at him and said — (*fixing his eyes on SIDNEY*) "The question is, Ralph, what are you doing — (*New England old-timer inflection*) out *thay-ah*?"

IRIS. (*knowing SIDNEY only too well and sensing the drift, starts exaggeratedly humming* "The Battle Hymn of the Republic")

SIDNEY. Cut it out.

ALTON. (*coolly plunging in for the kill*) *Why*, Sid? She's right . . . Wally, stop that foolishness! You're "venerating the human spirit!" Sidney's "conscience" is showing and his readers don't want that. He cannot afford that — he's a businessman now. Let's go before he offers to sell you his glasses!

SIDNEY. (*stung*) Well, hooray the hell for you! . . . John the Baptist! (*throws himself on his knees in a slow and very bored salaam*) God bless your selfless, selfless soul! (*Hands fluttering holy-roller style, he begins a wailing chant.*) He has come! He has come to deliver us!

(*The last words peter out as ALTON stands over him relentless.*)

ALTON. Look out, man, you're getting "overinvolved." "Too emotional!" You've already paid your dues—shed your tears, right? After all, what was Willie Johnson to you? Only one kid? One lousy junkie all of fifteen. (*brutally off-hand*) What'd he do, sweep the floor at Walden Pond?

SIDNEY. I did what I could—

ALTON. Sure, Sid. I'll tell his mother.

IRIS. (*furious, pleading to hold back the inevitable*) Sidney, you gave him a job—you can't be responsible for every strange kid that walks in off the street!

SIDNEY. I tried to help.

ALTON. Let's go, Wally, we're wasting time. (*pulling WALLY after him*)

WALLY. (*pausing at the door*) I'm counting on you, Sid.

SIDNEY. Don't! (*They exit. There is a long pregnant beat as SIDNEY stands looking after them. IRIS's eyes are at once rivetted to him from the counter, where she is slicing salad, and they do not leave him. SIDNEY takes down the poster and puts it aside, wanders to drawing board, but the poster continues to draw him like a magnet. He picks up banjo and strums for a moment in thought. He props poster on coffee table, regards it, again puts it aside, stands looking out of window, then picks it up and—at last—turns hesitantly to IRIS.*) Iris, do you think maybe Wally really—

IRIS. (*as their eyes meet, knife poised in air over salad*) Sidney, I swear to heaven, I'LL POISON YOU!!!

BLACKOUT

SCENE 2

TIME: *Dusk. The following week.*

AT RISE: *ALTON and MAX are staring at a large canvas, propped with back to the audience in the rocker. MAX is by all odds an original: middle-aged, gravel-voiced, immutable in style and conviction, unshakable of ego, gruffly masculine, and physically—whether black* or white, round, tall or squat—a comic type unto himself. He wears sandals, stained jeans, turtleneck, colorful cigar, and a pained expression. ALTON bends sideways to left, then right, for another view, then advances, turns the painting upside down and steps back. MAX restores it right-side up. ALTON throws up his hands and walks away.*

ALTON. Damn, Max.

MAX. (*following him; irate*) Damn, hell! Alton, your main problem is you are a lit-er-al-ist. You were born a literalist and you will die a literalist. Up to your ass in reality!

ALTON. But, Max, a little reality in a painting is not such a bad—

MAX. And don't give me the Renaissance. I don't care how much time Michelangelo spent on the Sistine Chapel, he was wasting his time, dig? Fuck Michelangelo! Fuck Rembrandt! And fuck Da Vinci!

ALTON. But Max! Max, don't you think—

MAX. And you know what you can do with *Adam*'s finger! (*Imitating the extended hand in Michelangelo's* The Creation of Adam, *he abruptly thrusts up the "fin-*

---

*Note this casting possibility.

ger" with a raucous whistle.) They were earthbound, baby. Earth*bound*!

ALTON. Look, whether you recognize it or not there is a world out there, and the artist has a responsibility to try to reflect—

MAX. (*interrupting*) —*himself*! That's what you'll never understand, Alton. *That*'s the revolution!

ALTON. (*incredulous*) *This* is the revolution, Max? (*Picking up the painting, he turns it around and we see it for the first time.**)

MAX. (*snatching it back*) It's as close to the revolution as you'll ever get!

ALTON. The hell it is! Look, man—

MAX. Ssshhh. (*admiring it, almost reverentially*) It's heavy, man. (*As ALTON reaches for it, he withdraws it fastidiously.*) If you can't dig it, don't soil it, jack!

ALTON. (*as calmly and reasonably as he can manage*) Max, all I am saying is that obscurity is not the deepest damn thing going, you know? It's confused—so, like, it's supposed to be pro*found*? Well, it's one hell of a revolution if no one can tell what you're revolting about!

MAX. I'm not trying to *tell* anybody anything.

ALTON. (*nodding*) And you are definitely succeeding. But now you take Goya, for example. Or Charles White's Harlem. Or Van Gogh. Take Breughel—

MAX. Breughel! (*outraged gesture of the streets*) Back to the fucking Renaissance! Alton, you don't know a damn thing except *poster* art!

(*SIDNEY enters* D.R. *carrying a large banner.*)

---

*One hopes the designer will have a field day with this—as far-out as he can take it—but in whatever direction, it should be conceived for instantaneous audience impact.

SIDNEY. I got it.

ALTON. Great. I've already got the nails in.

(*SIDNEY flings one end to ALTON and they hold it for a moment unfurled. It reads* "O'HARA FOR REFORM." *They stride to window—where, presently, it hangs, face out to the street. The sign should be painted on fabric that permits the words to show through in reverse, dimly or sharply, as lit.*)

SIDNEY. All right, let's go to work. (*sits at his board, ALTON at his side*) Max, the new masthead!

MAX. (*He rises ceremoniously with his portfolio, draws out a posterboard and places it before them. Then, with a flourish, he flips back the coversheet to unveil his creation, and stands back, modestly.*) Just a rough idea, you know. (*SIDNEY and ALTON squint at it hard, look at each other, bewildered; they turn it sideways. MAX restores it. Finally, ALTON points to the bottom of the page.*)

SIDNEY. (*leaning down to peer at it*) *Ten-point* type for the name of the newspaper? At the bottom of the page? Who's going to see it?

MAX. (*Columbus Incarnate, Galileo, Copernicus, the Wright Brothers and Frank Lloyd in one.*) That's the whole point. You put it far right and low in the big field —and the eye *has* to follow. (*Professor to slow pupil. As the two lean in close, he grandly guides their eyes with a finger: across and down the page, from right to left, in a descending spiral that ends with a final thrust at the target at bottom. ALTON and SIDNEY, eye to eye, look at each other in silence, at last rise. MAX is offended, grabs the masthead and gathers his things.*)

SIDNEY. Max, I like it—it just occurred to me I like it!

MAX. Look, I thought it was something different, something fresh!

SIDNEY. But, Max—

MAX. It's always that way. You revolutionaries are all the same. You start out full of fire and end up full of . . . shit! (*He stamps out the door, SIDNEY jumps up to follow.*)

ALTON. (*by the sleeve*) No, Sidney! It looks like a bunch of art majors from Music and Art High School designed that page.

SIDNEY. (*breaking free*) Alton, will you please—! (*follows MAX out and* D.R.—*takes the masthead, studies it*) Max, it's so creative. You've done it again!

MAX. (*one more moment of immovable glory, then relents*) As a matter of fact, Sid, let's change it every week. (*SIDNEY and MAX go back in and cross to the board.*) You know, a different typeface—Old English, Gothic, Bodoni . . . (*inspired*) However we *feel* the day we're making it up!

SIDNEY. (*hopefully*) Sometimes a little bigger?

MAX. And in a different place! Locate it on a different place on the sheet every week!

ALTON. (*suddenly shouting*) It's a newspaper! It's a goddamn newspaper—not an avant-garde toy!

MAX. You know, once you've had that Marxist monkey on your back you're hooked for life! To Alton, a newspaper's not an aesthetic adventure, it's— (*raising clenched fist*) a weapon! (*He snatches up a shirt and leaps on couch to wave the banner of revolution with both hands as he sings the Communist anthem,* "The International."*)

"'Tis the final conflict
Let each stand in his place—
The international working class—"

---

*See p. 136.

ALTON. Aw, go to hell.

MAX. (*singing*)

"... Shall lead the human race!"

(*During this IRIS has come on,* D.R. *Now she halts in the door at the sight of MAX on couch, et al. She is in her uniform, carrying paella in a paper bag, a letter clutched in her mouth. SIDNEY takes it.*)

IRIS. (*facetious delight—not at all pleased to see them*) Well, *company*! And who have I invited to supper tonight?

ALTON. Paella?

IRIS. (*She nods "yes" with eyes closed, knowing that he will stay now. He puts his hand in the air to affect the classroom mannerism of a child.*) Max?

MAX. (*still on couch*) Paella. Like crazy. (*remembering suddenly; conflicted*) But the problem is . . . there's this chick I was supposed to meet—(*glances at watch*) Jesus, an hour ago . . .

SIDNEY. There it is. The primeval decision: food or sex! (*MAX closes his eyes to imagine, presumably, a little of each in turn: rubbing stomach with one hand, voluptuously weighing "sex" with the other.*)

ALTON. (*going and leaning under MAX to study the decision close-up*) And let us watch *primitive* man decide— (*MAX opens his eyes with a glint—the sex hand has triumphed. He steps down from the couch with unmistakable intent and grabs up his things.*) The *loins* triumph! See, Max, you're not a true primitive or you would have put *food* first! You only *paint* like a savage! (*pursuing MAX to door as IRIS takes the letter she had come in with from SIDNEY and exits into bedroom*) And where the hell did you get that outfit, man? You look just like a put-up job for Life-Magazine-Visits-the-Left-Bank.

MAX. (*A beat as he studies ALTON. Then:*) That's the difference between me and you, Alton: I have finally become a truly free man. I have even stopped worrying about *not* trying to look like a nonconformist *not* nonconforming. (*chucks his chin*) Dig? (*ALTON, conceding, extends hand, palm up, and MAX gives him some "skin," turns and exits, across* D.L., *triumphant, singing.*)

"Hey, pretty Mama!
Roll me in your big brass bed . . ."

(*ALTON takes the banjo down, crosses to the rocker and begins to pluck it. IRIS re-enters in jeans and a sweater, reading the letter.*)

IRIS. Why, Alton Scales . . . Gloria says that you asked her to marry you.

ALTON. She put it in writing?

SIDNEY. (*looks up at him and then at his wife*) You're that gone on her?

ALTON. (*sudden lover's hoarse sincerity*) In fact, I figure that if that babe doesn't get herself back here—like I could flip.

SIDNEY. I'll be damned. (*to his wife*) You never know.

IRIS. (*in astonishment*) You never know.

SIDNEY. What did she say?

ALTON. She didn't. She said she'd think about it while she was away— (*strumming out an accompaniment on banjo for emphasis*) —and like I have been *living* with tension for two weeks! (*Abruptly, his strum breaks into a song and he sings, but after a few lines, stops as the silence dawns on him. Tensely:*) What's the matter? (*Silence; SIDNEY re-concentrates on his board; IRIS just *sits, not knowing what to say. ALTON, tightly, with mounting anger:*) I said what's the matter, god-dammit! Come on, let's have it out, my little gray friends! This is like the moment of truth, old babies! Yeah, let's get to the nitty gritty, as it were!

IRIS. Oh, Alton!

SIDNEY. (*simply*) Why don't you take that damn tree off your shoulder? It's embarrassing. (*They glare at one another; ALTON softens.*)

ALTON. Baby, I have a right to think anything I want. In *this* world. Even of *you*, Sid.

SIDNEY. There are some misunderstandings that cost more than others, Alton.

IRIS. Besides, the point is—well, for crying out loud, who'd expect that you two? I mean: You're so Paul P. Proletarian and all, and she's Miss Madison Avenue.

ALTON. Well, hell, opposites attract, to coin a phrase. Besides, like— (*slowly, real slow*) I dig her! (*He has crossed back to rocker, sits.*)

SIDNEY. That much?

ALTON. *That* much.

SIDNEY. (*Russian accent*) Another revolutionary bites the dust.

IRIS. (*her eyes on him intently*) And that's *all* that we have to say about it, isn't it, Sidney?

SIDNEY. (*accepting it*) That's all.

IRIS. Where's my *Backstage*?

SIDNEY. (*back with his board*) Under the apples. (*She crosses to counter, finds and opens* Backstage.)

IRIS. (*a long afterthought*) And I don't like that expression, come to think of it.

SIDNEY. What expression?

IRIS. (*shaking her finger, not serious*) About biting the dust. On behalf of my Cherokee grandfather, I protest!

ALTON. I got your point, so knock it off!

IRIS. (*turning on him*) You knock it off, sometimes, Alton! It's a bore! You and the causes all the time! It's phony as hell.

ALTON. (*in kind*) I was born with *this* cause!

IRIS. That's what I mean! Fun with illusion and reality: white boy playing black boy all the time.

ALTON. I *am* a black boy. I didn't make up the game.

IRIS. (*pragmatic bohemia*) But the country is full of people who dropped it when they could—what makes you so ever-loving different?

ALTON. It's something you either understand or you don't understand.

SIDNEY. Right! This is a stupid conversation. Be a *Martian* if you wanna.

ALTON. (*Boiling over, he rises and heads for the door.*) Yeah. Thanks, Sid. I'll try that sometime!

IRIS. Alton—

ALTON. (*Halts in the door, gets hold of himself; he turns, measuring them.*) Look . . . Sid, Iris, if I didn't love you— (*A beat. How to bridge the unbridgeable?*) I know. *You* don't care if I'm— (*ironically: with all the blandness of the old catchphrase*) "blue, green, purple or polka-dot," right? (*IRIS nods innocently. SIDNEY, knowing better, says nothing. Evenly:*) Yeah, well, like —you *think* about that sometime. 'Cause those don't happen to be the options. (*a beat; shrugs, smiles*) I'm going out for some wine for the feed. Want anything? Cigarettes?

SIDNEY. (*grinning*) Nope.

ALTON. How about you, Laughing Tomahawk? (*He saunters out.*)

IRIS. Flowers. For the table. (*follows him out the door and* D.R., *calling after him*) If you're going to be a brother-in-law you should try to get in with me. Bring me flowers every day . . . (*at the top of her lungs*) Lumumba!!! (*She ducks as the paperback he has been reading comes crashing against the door-frame; comes back in, at once.*) You just keep your mouth shut about Gloria, you hear!

SIDNEY. Did I say anything?

IRIS. No, but you sat there looking like death. Let them work it out, see!

SIDNEY. (*almost screaming, as the point has been made*) Did I say anything, did I say anything, *shrew*?

IRIS. (*on couch, turning back to her paper*) No, but I know you! The world's biggest busybody. (*SIDNEY gets up, crosses, hands her the new masthead and, like the cat that swallowed the canary, unveils it with the same proud flourish of the coversheet as MAX. IRIS sits blankly, squints, looks at SIDNEY, turns it sideways and upside down. Undeterred, he rights it and guides her eye in almost exact repetition of MAX's earlier demonstration. A beat, then squinting close:*) You keeping it a secret? Looks arty.

SIDNEY. (*furious*) All right—so it looks "arty." What does that mean, do you know?

IRIS. Do I know what?

SIDNEY. Do you know what "arty" means? Or is it just some little capsule phrase you zing out to try to diminish me, since you have nothing genuinely analytical or even observant to say?

IRIS. I wasn't trying to be analytical. I was saying what I thought—which is that it looks arty.

SIDNEY. You mean it looks different from other publications.

IRIS. No, I mean that it looks— (*dictionary definition, teacher to very slow pupil*) different from other publications in a *self-conscious* sort of way. *Art-tee.*

SIDNEY. Iris, where did you get the idea you know enough about these things to pass judgment on them?

IRIS. From the same place you got the idea that you were an editor.

SIDNEY. Which happens at least to be more reasonable than the idea that *you* are anybody's ACTRESS!

IRIS. (*putting down her paper, slowly, hurtfully*) Why don't you just hit me with your fist sometimes, Sid? (*Exits into bathroom; sobs are heard.*)

SIDNEY. I didn't mean that, baby. Come on. Do *South Pacific.*

IRIS. No. (*more sobs*)

SIDNEY. Iris, honey, come on . . . I'll hold the book for you. (*He opens the door—she pulls it shut. He tries again and she, clutching the knob, is tugged into the room.*)

IRIS. (*crossing away*) Why should I go through all of that to read for something that I know I won't get in the first place? They don't want actresses, they just want—(*loftily, making a production of it*) —EASY LAYS, that's all!! (*snarling*) That Harry Maxton, *please*! He's the biggest lech of them all! (*Pause; then, as the idea strikes her:*) You want to know something? You really want to hear something I hope will burn your little ears off? *That*'s why I didn't get the part before. (*sits grandly*) *I said "NO"!!* (*crosses her legs triumphantly and looks dead out front*)

SIDNEY. (*Long pause as he absorbs it; then—quietly, almost gently:*) Iris . . . everybody knows that Harry Maxton is one of the most famous *fags* in America.

IRIS. (*a beat; with a wild, cornered look*) All right then. So everything goes with him! He just—he just puts on the fag bit to cover up what he *really* is!—(*He turns away, embarrassed for her. She pushes on desperately.*)

Well, that's how twisted up they are in show business!

SIDNEY. (*understated*) Iris, honey, even in show business—*that* twisted they're not.

IRIS. Leave me alone, Sidney. I don't want the part. (*She has curled into a tight sulking ball in the rocker. Getting the book and then crossing back to her, he gently pulls her out of the rocker.*)

SIDNEY. Oh, Iris, Iris, Iris . . . (*He puts his head wearily on her breast.*) I want to help . . . so much . . . I'm on your side.

IRIS. I just don't have it. They say if you really have it—you stick with it no matter what—and that—that you'll do anything—

SIDNEY. That is one of the greatest, cruelest romantic myths in America. A lot of people "have it" and they just get trampled to death by the mob trying to get up the same mountain.

IRIS. Oh please, Sidney, don't start blaming everything on society. Sooner or later a person learns to hold *himself* accountable—that's what maturity is. If I haven't learned anything else in analysis—

SIDNEY. Thank you Dr. Steiner! Look, Iris, the world's finest swimmer cannot swim the Atlantic Ocean—even if analysis *does* prove it was his mother's fault!

IRIS. That's not an analogy. *Nobody* can swim the Atlantic Ocean—but some people *do* make it in the theatre. (*She smiles at him and settles into his arms.*) You make the lousiest analogies. Just like you can't add. I couldn't believe that at first.

SIDNEY. What?

IRIS. About your arithmetic. I thought you were putting me on. You know, anybody all *that* brilliant who couldn't *add*. God, at home almost *nobody* could read

—but *everybody* could add! (*playing with his hair a little*) Hey, Sidney. How much is one and zero?

SIDNEY. Zero. One.

IRIS. Oh, very good. And one and one?

SIDNEY. One and one is two.

IRIS. And seven and seven?

SIDNEY. Fourteen, naturally.

IRIS. (*quickly*) And fourteen and fourteen?

SIDNEY. (*Hesitates; she giggles.*) Twenty-eight.

IRIS. And twenty-eight and twenty-eight?

SIDNEY. (*abruptly lost*) Oh, c'mon. That's calculus . . . (*Both laugh, embrace.*)

IRIS. You don't know what it's like though. (*She is looking off, moving her fingers through his hair.*) God, to walk through those agency doors! There's always some gal sitting at a desk, you know, with a stack of pictures practically up to the ceiling. And she's always bored, you know. (*looking at him*) I mean even the nice ones, they've seen five million and two like you and by the time you come through the door they are *bored.* (*rises and starts to dramatize*) And when you get past them, into the waiting room, there they are—the five million and two sitting there waiting—and they look just as scared and mean and competitive as you do. And so you all sit there, and you don't know anything: how you look, how you feel, anything. And least of all—how they want you to *read.* And when you get inside, you know less. There are just those faces. Christ, you almost wish someone *would* make a pass or something: you could deal with that—that's from *life.* But that almost never happens, at least not to me. All I ever see are those blank director-producer-writer faces just staring, waiting for you to *show* them something, *excite* them. And you just stand there knowing that you *can't*—no matter what, you can't *do* it the way you did it at home in front of the mirror—the brilliant, imaginative way you did it the night before. And all you can think is: what the hell am I doing here in front of these strangers, reading these silly words and jumping around for that fairy like some kind of NUT. . . ! (*escaping back to the shelter of his embrace*) Oh, Sidney, this is all a waste of time. You know and I know I will never show up for that audition. I just don't want to see those faces again—oh Jesus, do I ever feel *twenty-nine*!

SIDNEY. Sure you will, honey. (*She shakes her head.*) I'll help you. (*She takes the book out of his hand, takes hold of him and they kiss.*) Take down your hair for me, Iris . . .

IRIS. (*hoarsely, but not angrily*) Christ, you're still so hooked on my hair . . . (*laughter through tears*) It's spooky to be loved for your hair, don't you know that?

SIDNEY. Take down your hair . . . (*He reaches up and pulls the pins and it falls and there really is a great deal of it which almost covers her. Then he gets up and puts on a RECORD and turns and waits: a stinging mountain banjo hoedown cuts into the silence. It swells and races, filling room and theatre.*) Dance for me, Iris Parodus. Come down out of the hills and dance for me, Mountain Girl!

IRIS. (*lifting up her eyes to him*) I just don't feel Appalachian tonight, Sid! It just won't work tonight—

SIDNEY. Why not, Mountain Girl?

IRIS. (*turning off PHONOGRAPH*) Sidney . . . I am not your mountain girl anymore. (*Then quickly:*) I'm sorry. I really am. I've changed on you, haven't I? The things you don't know about me! Like, for example, my hair—

SIDNEY. (*clowning*) It's—a WIG??!

IRIS. Idiot! I mean the only reason I wear it like this is because of you— (*He smiles delighted.*) I *hate* my hair this way.

SIDNEY. You do?

IRIS. (*shaking her head with wonder*) I didn't always. When I first came here, you know, I was working, dancing in this little nothing of a sawed-off club. And one of the girls, after listening to me run on, said: "Well, honey, if *that*'s the kind of man you want, you've gotta go down to the Black Knight Tavern and sit." (*smiling*) "Let your hair grow long and go to the Black Knight Tavern." Sounds like a folksong. So that's what I did, and—there you were! You, Alton and Max—"holding forth." And I said to myself, "There's the one!" And the next day I started eating vitamins, like this same girl said, to make my hair grow faster. So help me God, *vitamins*! I dunno, Sid. Everything seemed so simple then . . . (*deep in thought*) I just wanted to go, do, be whatever you wanted, to . . . to . . .

SIDNEY. To what, Iris?

IRIS. I guess just to *please* you, Sid.

SIDNEY. And that's a bad thing?

IRIS. I don't know, Sid. I mean, like it just doesn't seem to work anymore—no matter how I try . . . and I want . . .

SIDNEY. . . . What? What is it you want, Iris Parodus?

IRIS. God, I wish I knew. (*a beat*) I suppose a part of me wants it to be the way it used to be. Sidney, I couldn't believe it—that *you* should love *me*! I felt I was the luckiest girl in the world—

SIDNEY. What do you mean "was"? (*Playfully reaching for her; she responds.*)

IRIS. (*nuzzling him*) Sidney. Please. I'm trying to tell you something.

SIDNEY. I'm trying to listen.

IRIS. Try harder. (*kisses him*) I love you, Sidney Brustein. I love you, silly—sweet—stinker Sidney Brustein. (*looking into his eyes*) But it's not enough.

SIDNEY. For me it's plenty.

IRIS. (*getting up*) Yes, I know. That's sort of the problem . . . (*She turns to face him and they look at each other; a beat.*)

SIDNEY. (*mugging to disguise his unease*) "Problem"? What problem?! (*crosses swiftly to turn RECORD on*) Tomorrow we'll just start spiking your paella with *vitamins*! Now, c'mon, Mountain Girl, dance!

IRIS. (*hurling pillow*) Sidney, you're hopeless!

SIDNEY. (*clapping and stamping his feet as the hoedown soars*) You betcha sweet ass I am!

(*During this MAVIS BRYSON has entered,* D.R. *She is a heavier, red-headed version of IRIS, more uptown and fashionable. She knocks and IRIS opens door —then, as swiftly, shuts and bars it with her outstretched arms and body, her back to door.*)

IRIS. (*meaning the dress box her sister is carrying*) I don't want it, I don't need it, and I won't take it!

MAVIS. (*through door*) Just try it on. That's all I ask. (*IRIS reluctantly admits her.*) Hello, Sid, darling.

SIDNEY. Hello, Mav. (*He crosses to the bar, selects an apple from basket.*)

MAVIS. (*blithely opens the box and holds dress up*) Could we conceivably have the hootennany at another time? (*crosses to PHONOGRAPH and turns off the RECORD*)

IRIS. We don't go to cocktail parties, Mavis. At least the kind where you dress like *that*. I want to tell you from the top, Mavis. I am in no mood for the big sister-little sister hassle today— (*MAVIS maternally stops IRIS's mouth in mid-speech with one hand.*)

MAVIS. Just slip it on. You'll look stunning in it. I had it taken up for you. (*confidentially, as she zips and buttons*) What's that awful sign? Iris, it looks so vulgar to have writing in your window. What have you heard from Gloria?

IRIS. Not a word.

MAVIS. Here, let me smooth it down on you. Now, really, I can't tell a thing with those sticking out. (*IRIS pulls up her jeans as far as possible under the dress.*) It's stunning! Now, all you'll need for Easter is a new pair of sneakers.

SIDNEY. (*appreciatively*) You're coming along, Mavis, you're coming along. How's about a drink? (*He goes to the bar.*)

MAVIS. You know, you're drinking a lot lately, Sidney. (*She does a take as she sees the glasses. To Iris:*) I thought you always said that the Jews didn't drink.

SIDNEY. (*broadly, raising whole bottle*) Mavis, I'm assimilated! (*Drinks, tilts head back and gargles; IRIS exits into bedroom.*)

MAVIS. (*calling after her*) Where was Gloria when you heard from her?

IRIS. (o.s.) Miami Beach— (*popping her head out*) And you're turning into a pure sneak—! (*withdraws again*)

MAVIS. And you weren't going to tell me. (*to SIDNEY*) Why can't she tell me? Miami Beach, my God! Is she still—? (*SIDNEY nods up and down slowly:* "what else?" *MAVIS covers her eyes.*) Oh, the poor baby. You know, Sidney, when she was little she wanted to be a sailor. Isn't that funny? She was so tiny and feminine and she said, "When I grow up I'll be the first girl sailor in the whole world!" She was so determined . . . And now all I can think of is I'm so glad Papa didn't live to—

IRIS. (*re-enters pinning her hair up—sans dress*) Look, Mavis, don't start. I just don't want the Gloria problem tonight. No matter what else—she is living *her* life and we are living *ours*. (*dryly, as SIDNEY toasts her brightly*) So to speak.

MAVIS. (*to SIDNEY*) Is she coming any time soon? (*He immediately starts nodding* "yes." *IRIS, behind her back, angrily signals him,* "no." *In mid-nod SIDNEY switches from "yes" to "no." MAVIS turns to IRIS.*)

IRIS. She didn't say.

MAVIS. When?

IRIS. Mavis, if you weren't the world's greatest living anti-Semite you really should have married Sidney so that the two of you— (*joining their hands in wedlock*) could have minded the world's business together! Jees!

MAVIS. That's not funny and I am not, for the four thousandth time, an anti-Semite. *You* don't think that about me, do you, Sid, *why*? (*Taking the answer for granted, she does not even look at SIDNEY. There is no pause at all between the statement and the* "why.")

SIDNEY. (*He starts to whistle* Exodus.)

MAVIS. (*whirls to face him*) *Why?*

IRIS. Now, come on: you nearly had a heart attack when we got married. In fact, *that*'s when you went into analysis. Now either you were madly in love with *me* or you hate the Jews—pick! (*MAVIS jumps up and crosses* DS. *as SIDNEY and IRIS toast.*)

MAVIS. Sometimes, Iris . . . (*a beat*) Did she say if she needs anything?

IRIS. Now, what could she need? She's the— (*wiggle of the hips or lewd wink*) successful one!

MAVIS. Iris, you've gotten to be just plain dirty-minded.

IRIS. Look, we happen to have a sister who is a fancy call girl, a big-time, high-fashion *whore.* (*breezily to both of them*) And I say so what? She's wracking up THOUSANDS of *tax-free* dollars a year and it's her life so—who's to say? (*Having done with responsibility, she shrugs with confidence.*)

MAVIS. How can you talk like that—it's your baby sister! (*sits on couch opposite SIDNEY*) Sidney, Gloria's a sick girl. She's not bad. She's very, very sick.

IRIS. Look, Mav, you're all hung up in the puritan ethic. That's not my problem.

MAVIS. Is anything?

IRIS. It's an anti-sex society—

SIDNEY. (*Exploding: enough is enough.*) Will you shut up! I can't stand it when you start prattling every lame-brained libertarian slogan that comes along without knowing what the hell you are talking about!

IRIS. (*advancing indignantly*) I am entitled to my opinion, Sid-nee!

SIDNEY. No, you are *not*! (*They are jaw-to-jaw across MAVIS.*) Not so long as your opinion is based on stylish ignorance!

IRIS. Oh, shut up, Sidney! On the subject of sex you are the last of the Victorians! (*turning on her heel and back to the rocker*)

SIDNEY. Not at all. The Victorians, sweet, were not against sex, sin or prostitution. They were opposed to their *visibility*!

IRIS. Well, who cares! My whole point is it's an anti-sex society—

SIDNEY. Look, Iris, love— (*He grabs his head with frustration.*) How can I put it to you—in front of Mavis here— There ought to be some human relationships on which commerce cannot put its grisly paws, doncha think?

MAVIS. (*her voice rising above them*) The *things* you people *think* you have to talk about!

SIDNEY. (*eyes lighting as he and IRIS eye MAVIS; cat and mouse*) Oh, Iris . . . why don't you tell her the new development?

MAVIS. (*turning to him very slowly*) What?

IRIS. (*to SIDNEY*) Fat mouth.

MAVIS. (*wheeling to her sister*) What—? (*advancing vehemently*) What what WHAT??

IRIS. (*with a grudging look at SIDNEY*) There's somebody we know who wants to marry her.

MAVIS. (*closing her eyes and leaning back as if a prayer had been answered*) Praise his name! (*SIDNEY, smiling angelically, crosses closer, studying her. Abruptly she sobers.*) Who? (*anticipating the worst*) One of *your* friends? (*He nods "yes" and she, frowning, nods with him. Then:*) What does he . . . *do*?

SIDNEY. Well, as a matter of fact, he works in a bookstore.

MAVIS. In a *what*?

SIDNEY. A place where they sell books. (*She winces, weighs and accepts it:* "It could be worse." *Then:*) Part time. (*She stares at him.*) And as a matter of fact he used to be a Communist. (*The last straw: as his open-mouthed sister-in-law is on the point of exploding, he raises one hand reassuringly.*) But it's all right, Mav. He's strictly an— (*enunciating each letter*) N.M.S.S.-type Red.

MAVIS. What kind is that?

SIDNEY. (*Russian accent*) "No-more-since-Stalin."

MAVIS. Does he know? (*SIDNEY stares at her innocently.*) Does he know what—ah . . . ?

SIDNEY. (*helping her at last*) What Gloria *does*? For a *living*? No. She told him the model bit.

MAVIS. (*hopefully*) Listen, people like that, I mean Communists and things—they're supposed to be very *radical* . . . about things . . . well . . . (*pathetically*) Well, aren't they?

SIDNEY. Who can say? There's— (*profoundly: measuring the words as if he were saying something really weighty, while she hangs upon every word*) "people like that" . . . and "people like—that . . ." (*As she strains forward eagerly, he abruptly lets the last word drop innocuously, leaving her hanging.*)

MAVIS. (*a beat; then:*) Is he good-looking? What about Gloria? What does she . . . (*rising, ecstatic as she finally sees it: the shower, the caterer, invitation list, honeymoon arrangements*) Oh, I *knew* this nightmare would have to end! (*pacing back and forth,* DS.)

SIDNEY. Uh, Mavis . . .

MAVIS. It was just something that happened. It's the way the world is these days . . .

SIDNEY. (*casually, sneaking it in*) He's also a Negro one, Mavis.

MAVIS. People just don't know what to do with— (*As it hits her she freezes and hangs there; deep, guttural.*) A *NEGRO WHAT*—??

SIDNEY. (*simple answer to a simple question*) A Negro Communist. (*She turns helplessly toward IRIS. Then:*) Well, that is to say, he's not a Communist anymore. (*Pause; she looks at him.*) But he's still a Negro.

MAVIS. (*looking from one to the other*) Are you—Are you sitting there talking about a . . . a . . . *colored* boy?

SIDNEY. (*rapidly, wagging his finger*) 1964, Mavis, 1964! "Uncommitted Nations!" "Free World." Don't say it, honey, don't say it! We'll think you're not . . . chic!

MAVIS. Well, I don't think you're funny worth a damn! What do you think Gloria *IS*—?! (*She turns abruptly away, trapped: what Gloria "is" is hardly her trump card. Indignantly:*) Well, if this is your idea of some kind of bohemian joke I just don't think it's cute or clever or *anything*! I would rather see her—

SIDNEY. —go on shacking up with any poor sick bastard in the world with a hundred bucks for a convention weekend!? (*They glare at one another.*)

MAVIS. (*furious*) Well now, listen, there are *other* men in the world! The last time I looked around me there were still some *white* men left in this world! Some fine ordinary upstanding plain decent very white men who were still looking to marry very white women . . .

(*During the above DAVID RAGIN has descended the stairway from his apartment overhead; now he pushes open the door and saunters in. An intense, slim, studied young man, casually dressed, his mannerisms suggesting the entirely unmannered—but by choice. DAVID's bearing is neither virile nor, in the least, "swish." He is not sophomoric, but a genuine intellectual. He can be at times cuttingly aloof and untouchable, yet at others quite likeable in the vulnerability he labors to conceal. Despite his running debate with SIDNEY, between the two lurks genuine affection.*)

IRIS. Why hello, David. David Ragin, this is my sister, Mrs. Bryson.

MAVIS. (*composing herself*) How do you do?

DAVID. (*barely acknowledging her; to IRIS*) You have any paper?

IRIS. Bedroom. (*DAVID exits into it and MAVIS turns to her curiously.*)

MAVIS. Well, *he*'s sort of cute.

IRIS. David is a playwright who lives upstairs. (*quite matter-of-factly*) And *we* are the government – and we subsidize him.

MAVIS. (*to SIDNEY*) Is he married?

SIDNEY. Not in *your* terms. (*MAVIS peers at him puzzled.*) David's got an alternative lifestyle. (*MAVIS considers but doesn't get it.*) David's gay. (*She still doesn't.*) Queer.

IRIS. Homosexual. (*MAVIS draws back.*)

SIDNEY. Utterly.

MAVIS. Oh. (*afterthought*) Well, maybe she would want a rest. (*DAVID re-enters.*) Well, I should get on. (*as she pulls on her gloves*) What are you writing, young man?

DAVID. Nothing you'd be interested in.

SIDNEY. (*a gleam in his eye*) Go on tell her about your play, David. There is nothing else she can hear that's shocking today.

DAVID. Cool it, Sidney.

SIDNEY. (*grandly*) David is engaged in the supreme effort of trying to wrest the theatre from the stranglehold of Ibsenesque naturalism, are you not, David? (*DAVID stares indifferently at them.*) As a matter of fact he has a play in production right now.

MAVIS. Oh, how nice! Is there something in it for Iris?

IRIS. (*exploding*) Mavis, you're not supposed to do that.

MAVIS. Why not . . . ?

SIDNEY. Besides, there are only two characters in David's play. And they are both male and they are both married. To each other. (*a beat*) And the entire action of the play takes place in the refrigerator.

MAVIS. (*does a slow take and edges off a little*) I see.

DAVID. *I* didn't try to tell you what it was about.

SIDNEY. Then tell *me*. What *is* your play about, David?

DAVID. It's not for me to say.

SIDNEY. Each person will "get from it what he brings to it?" Right?

DAVID. To be real simple-minded about it—yes.

SIDNEY. Then, what makes *you* the artist and the *audience* the consumer if *they* have to write your play for you?

DAVID. *I* know what it's about. (*SIDNEY merely looks at him.*) I told you, my plays have to speak for themselves.

SIDNEY. But to *whom*? For whom are they written and, above all, *why* are they written?

MAVIS. (*who has been turning from one to the other throughout, fascinated, and trying all the while to get a word in edgewise*) I just don't know whatever happened to simple plays about simple people with simple problems. (*Both turn to regard her and then resume without comment.*)

DAVID. All I can say is that I write because I have to and what I have to. Whatever you think of it, Sidney, *I write.* I squeeze out my own juices and offer them up. I may be afraid, but *I* write. (*They stare at each other.*)

MAVIS. Well, that's nice . . . (*They stare at her.*) Well, got to meet Fred. Did I tell you the news, Iris? Fred's been put in charge of the Folk River Dam Project, now what do you think of that? (*She beams.*)

IRIS. I think we are a talented family, obviously. Success in whatever we put our— (*suggestive wriggle—to outrage*) *hands* to.

MAVIS. Iris, not in front of people!

IRIS. David isn't people, he's a writer. And he worships

prostitutes. He says they are the only *real* women—the core of life, as it were. Don't you, David? (*He ignores this.*)

MAVIS. The only thing about your flippancies, Iris, is that they don't solve any problems.

SIDNEY. (*who has been suddenly struck by what Fred's finances might mean to him*) So old Fred is really doing all right for himself, huh?

IRIS. Look out, Mavis, you're about to be tapped—

SIDNEY. You!

MAVIS. (*pleasantly*) Now Sidney, you know Fred won't invest in a nightclub.

IRIS. The nightclub is dead. Long live the newspaper!

SIDNEY. *It wasn't a nightclub*—

MAVIS. A newspaper? (*great intake of breath and, immediately, laughter*) Oh, Sidney, Sidney, Sidney! When are you going to grow up. A *newspaper*?!

SIDNEY. Oh, forget it!

MAVIS. Well, I really must go. (*to her sister—softly*) You *will* let me know when Gloria is coming?

IRIS. (*a great sigh*) Mavis—sooner or later you are going to learn that Gloria is a big girl now and doesn't want us to play Mama. Live and let live! (*She crosses into the kitchen to fetch supper dishes.*)

MAVIS. That's just a shoddy little way to avoid responsibility in the world.

SIDNEY. (*bellowing*) Mavis—please *go*! It makes me *nervous* to be on your side!

MAVIS. I'm going, I'm going. (*as her eye catches the sign again*) And Sidney, you will take the sign down for —Passover? (*IRIS proceeds to lay out dishes on coffee table.*)

DAVID. (*looking at it*) And what have you got against the "machine" *this* week?

SIDNEY. It's a machine, David! With a boss!

DAVID. (*a little roused, finally*) Well, what is the virtue of getting one boss out and putting another one in?

SIDNEY. The virtue—the virtue, my dear boy, if you will pardon the rhetoric, is to participate in some expression of the people about the way things are.

MAVIS. Well, Fred always says, when you come right down to it one politician is just like another.

DAVID. (*smiling and nodding toward MAVIS as specimen*) Sidney, don't you know yet that the "good guys" and "bad guys" went out with World War II?

SIDNEY. (*rocking with his hands in prayerful fashion*) Ah yes! And a new religion has arisen in the West! (*intoning a mock Mass*) "We are all guilty . . . Father Camus, we are all guilty . . . therefore all guilt is equal . . . therefore *no one* is guilty . . . therefore we can in clear conscience abstain from the social act . . . and even the social thought . . ."

DAVID. (*glaring at him*) Go ahead! Kid it. It's easier to kid it than face the pain in it.

SIDNEY. (*mugging—with vast exaggeration*) Ah, "*Pain*!" (*He clutches his side.*) "Pain in recognizing those dark tunnels which lead back to our primate souls! (*He rises to a half-stoop, arms dangling, and, ape-like, crosses up onto coffee table and then the sofa.*) The savage soul of man from whence sprang the Lord of the Flies, Beelzebub himself! Man, dark gutted creature of ancestral— (*leaping over the back of the sofa and lifting his hands in Bela Lugosi style*) cannibalism and all-consuming eeevil! Agghhh. (*Through the bars of the rocking chair he snarls and claws at all of them.*) Yahhh! The Shadow knows. (*subsides cowering there with tongue flicking defiantly*)

MAVIS. I just said to Fred this morning: "Say what you like, it's always something different down at Iris and Sid's." (*ALTON re-enters, from* D.R., *with paper bag and the flowers.*)

DAVID. Well, Fidel Castro, I presume.

ALTON. (*in kind*) Jean Genet, as I live and breathe. (*They shake.*)

SIDNEY. (*taking the wine*) Did you bottle it yourself?

IRIS. (*taking her flowers*) David, aren't you going to stay to eat?

DAVID. Why not?

IRIS. Mav?

MAVIS. No, dear! I've got to meet Fred. (*Reluctantly: her matchmaker eyes have not left ALTON since his entrance.*)

IRIS. Alton, I'd like you to meet my sister Mavis. Mavis, this is Alton Scales.

MAVIS. How do you do?

ALTON. How do you do. (*As he crosses, she stands admiring him.*)

MAVIS. (*to SIDNEY*) Is *he* married?

SIDNEY. No.

MAVIS. He isn't—ahhh— (*meaning homosexual*)

SIDNEY. We're not sure yet. (*Sits; all except MAVIS are now seated about coffee table.*)

MAVIS. (*a trill in her voice*) Good night, Mr. Scales.

ALTON. (*rises to help her on with her coat*) Good night. (*ALTON sits.*)

SIDNEY. (*abruptly, so that all hear him, as she starts out*) Oh, Mavis, this is the chap we were just telling you about. (*She looks blank.*) From the bookstore.

(*There is silence; ALL except DAVID know the meaning of the moment for MAVIS. They variously concentrate on the food and exchange superior and rather childish glances; letting her live through the moment of discomfort. She turns slowly around to face the youth again. It is a contemporary confrontation for which nothing in her life has prepared her. There is silence and much deliberate chewing and eye-rolling. ALTON is prepared for virtually anything—to smile and kiss and be kissed, to scream or be screamed at, or to be struck and strike back. Presently, this woman of conformist helplessness does the only thing she can, under these circumstances: she gags on her words so that they are hardly audible and repeats what she has already said.*)

MAVIS. Oh. How do you do.

ALTON. (*raising his eyes evenly*) How do you do.

(*He turns and reaches for the food. MAVIS stands thoughtfully, watching this table in bohemia, the random art of the setting: a huge leafy salad, a bottle of wine, some candles, thick European bread; a portrait of diners who would sit down together only here: the taciturn young homosexual; the young Negro who is to be a kinsman; her sister, seemingly at home here; her brother-in-law, who presides.*)

SIDNEY. (*as she heads for the door*) Well, Alton, now you have met Mavis. There she is: the Bulwark of the Republic. The Mother Middleclass itself standing there revealed in all her towering courage. (*There are snickers of delight; he has even perhaps lifted his wine glass.*) Mavis, go or stay—but we're eating. (*slapping at ALTON's paw*) One to a man! One to a man! (*MAVIS halts and turns to face them.*)

MAVIS. (*She is silent so long that they look up at her; still with varying degrees of amusement; then:*) I am standing here and I am thinking: how smug it is in bohemia. *I* was taught to believe that— (*near tears*) creativity and great intelligence ought to make one expansive and understanding. That if ordinary people, among whom I have the sense at least to count myself, could not expect understanding from artists and—whatever it is that *you* are, Sidney—then where indeed might we look for it at all—in this quite dreadful world. (*She almost starts out, but turns back for the cap.*) Since you have all so busily got rid of God for us! (*turns and exits,* D.R.)

IRIS. So— (*knocking him in the ribs*) put that in your pipe and smoke it, old dear!

DAVID. (*amused*) Some day I really must look into what it is that makes the majority so oppressively defensive.

ALTON. (*the most affected*) Oh quit it!

DAVID. (*turning on him*) And now the gentle heart of the oppressed will also admonish us.

ALTON. Turn off, Fag Face!

DAVID. (*puts down his fork*) Isn't it marvelous, some people have their Altons and some have their Davids. You should be grateful to the Davids of the world, Alton: we at least provide a distraction from the cross you so nobly and so *deliberately* bear! (*ALTON jumps up and heads for the door.*)

IRIS. Where are you going—?

ALTON. I'm sorry if it makes me unsophisticated in your eyes, but after a while, hanging out with queers gets on my nerves! (*ALTON slams out of the house* U.R., *as DAVID, ironically, blows him a kiss and trills out:*)

DAVID. 'Bye—! (*He sits on in silence.*)

IRIS. (*reaching out to him gently*) Eat your supper, David. Alton's a big kid.

DAVID. (*turning his eyes on her slowly, steadily; a trap, casually:*) *You* accept queers, don't you, Iris?

IRIS. (*innocent shrug*) Sure.

DAVID. Yes, because you accept *anything*. But—I am not *anything*. I hope he never has to explore the *why* of his discomfort!

SIDNEY. (*flaring suddenly*) Oh no . . . Come on, David! Don't start that jazz! Is that the best you can do? Is that really it? Anybody who attacks one—*is* one?!

IRIS. Sidney. Can't you be still sometimes . . . ?

SIDNEY. (*raising his hand in a definite "stop" sign*) I mean it, Iris. I am bored with the syndrome.

IRIS. Who cares!

SIDNEY. (*shouting at IRIS*) Is that all you can ever say? Who cares, who cares? Let the damn bomb fall if somebody wants to drop it! Well, I admit it: *I* care! I care about it all. It takes too much energy *not* to care! Yesterday I counted 26 gray hairs on the top of my head—all from trying *not* to care. And you, David, you have now written fourteen plays about not caring, about the isolation of the soul of man, the alienation of the human spirit, the desolation of all love, all possible communication. When what you really want to say is that you are ravaged by a society that will not sanctify your particular sexuality!

DAVID. It seems to have conveniently escaped your attention that *I* am the insulted party here.

SIDNEY. (*overbearingly*) If somebody insults you—sock 'im in the jaw! If you don't like the sex laws, attack 'em, I think they stink! You wanna get up a petition? I'll sign it. Love little fishes if you want! But, David, *please* get over the notion that your particular "thing" is something that only the deepest, saddest, most nobly tortured can know about. It ain't—(*spearing into the salad*) it's just one kind of sex—that's all. And, in my opinion—(*revolving his fork*) the universe turns regardless. (*DAVID *looks at him for a long moment, and then gets up and goes to the door.*)

IRIS. (*jumping up after DAVID*) What's the matter with everybody? David, come on, eat your supper.

DAVID. I prefer to eat alone. (*exits up the stairs*)

IRIS. (*closing the door*) Well, that was some dinner party, thank you. What's with you lately, Sidney? Why do you have to pick at everybody? Where did you get the idea it was up to you to improve everybody?

SIDNEY. (*in a fierce mood*) I don't try to improve everybody. Or, at least, you can't tell it by you!

IRIS. (*properly hurt*) All right, Sid, one of these days you've got to decide who you want—Margaret Mead or Joan Baez? I won't play both! As a matter of fact it's getting pretty clear—maybe I've got to decide, too.

SIDNEY. The least excuse and you haul up the old self-pitying introspection bit.

IRIS. (*through her teeth*) What makes you think anybody can live with your insults?

SIDNEY. The world needs insults!

IRIS. (*the last straw*) Sweet Heaven. (*She starts to clear the table.*)

SIDNEY. I'm sorry. (*moves to help; she rejects this*) Hey! There's a rally for Wally. You wanna come?

IRIS. I told you, don't expect me to get involved with that stuff!

SIDNEY. All right, all right. You wanna go over to the Black Knight and have a couple of beers.

IRIS. No, I do not want to go over to the Black Knight and have a couple of beers.

SIDNEY. Well, then, suppose *you* just come up with something, *anything* you would like to do. It will be your first achievement in this entire marriage.

IRIS. Jesus, what does it do for you, Sid? Picking at

me like that. Sometimes I think—sometimes I think . . . (*She stops. It is almost impossible to go on.*) Look, why don't you just go to your rally and leave poor old Iris alone? (*turns on the PHONOGRAPH*)

SIDNEY. (*grabs his jacket and heads for door, then halts, hand on the knob, flings his jacket to the floor—helpless; more to himself than to her:*) Leave "poor old Iris alone"—and watch her turn quietly and willingly into a vegetable!

IRIS. (*She sits on the window seat, looking off, into the street—as a haunting guitar cuts the silence. Softly, fighting back tears; not looking at him:*) It's getting different, Sidney, our fighting. Something's either gone out of it or come into it. I don't know which. But it's something that keeps me from wanting to make up with you a few hours later. That's bad, isn't it?

SIDNEY. Yeah, that's bad. (*He turns and looks at his wife; she is crying—then picks up his jacket and starts out.*)

IRIS. (*crying out*) Then let's put up a fight for it, Sidney! I mean it—let's fight like hell for it. (*He halts at the outer staircase and stands clutching the rail as his wife sits looking after him; the light fades on all but the two of them, and the voice of Joan Baez, singing* "All My Trials," *fills the darkening stage.*)

CURTAIN

ACT TWO

Scene 1

TIME: *Just before daybreak, next day.*

AT RISE: *The faint light of PRE-DAWN illumines the outside staircase landing, where SIDNEY sprawls in thought, arms underhead. The silence of the great sleeping city is accentuated by the occasional moan of a FOGHORN, the whirr of TIRES or clatter of a MILKTRUCK. The apartment is dark, except for the SIGN in the window half-lit from the street outside. SIDNEY picks up his banjo and begins to pick it. The melody seems surely drawn from that other world which ever beckons him—a wistful, throbbing mountain blues—and as he plays the LIGHTING shifts magically to create the "mountain" realm of his dreams. Gone is even the distant foghorn; he is no longer in the city. After several phrases of this, the MUSIC soars and quickens into a vibrant stinging hoedown on the loudspeakers.*

Out of the shadows the IRIS-OF-HIS-MIND appears: barefooted, with flowing hair and wisps of a mountain dress, * *dancing through walls as if they do not exist in a joyous montage of dance Americana: the dip for the oyster, the grand right and left, etc. He does not turn to look at her, for there is no need to: she exists in his mind's eye. At climax, she mounts the stairs, throws him a kiss, and flees. He sits on, spent, plucks idly at the instrument, as we hear un-*

---

* The dress should clearly be ethereal and unreal—wisps rather than a single fabric.

mistakable country sounds: CRICKETS, FROGS, perhaps an OWL. These sounds continue faintly, intermittently, throughout the rest of the scene. Suddenly a bright, realistic LIGHT comes on in the open bedroom doorway and the real IRIS enters, belting her robe, yawning and rubbing her eyes.

IRIS. Sid—? (*He does not reply or even hear her.*) Sidney? (*She switches on LAMP, opens door and leans out.*) What are you doing outside? You'll wake the neighbors.

SIDNEY. (*in the same unbroken reverie*) They can't hear me, Iris.

IRIS. Oh, Sidney, you're a nut. C'mon in, I'll make you some coffee. (*She fishes out cigarettes and lights one.*)

SIDNEY. No, come on up. Listen! Do you hear the brook? There is nothing like clear brook water at daybreak.

IRIS. (*charmed in spite of herself*) You'll catch cold, Sidney. It's too early for games. Come to bed.

SIDNEY. No, Iris. Come on up. (*She does, and kneels beside him. The LAMP and bedroom LIGHT dim inobtrusively.*) Look at the pines—look at the goddamn pines. You can almost taste 'em. There's not another soul for miles, and if you listen, *really* listen—you might almost hear yourself think.

IRIS. (*surveying the realm, gently laughing*) This is some mountain.

SIDNEY. (*playful proprietary pride*) It's a small mountain—but it's ours.

IRIS. (*smiling*) *Yours*, Sidney.

SIDNEY. (*fondling her hair*) "Nymph in . . . all . . . my Orisons remembered." (*He kisses her and for a moment the MUSIC comes up and she enters fully into his dream. The inside LIGHTS fade out.*)

IRIS. (*looking up at him thoughtfully*) It really gets to you, doesn't it? You'd like to live right here, in the woods, wouldn't you? (*SIDNEY nods.*) And you're afraid to ask me, aren't you? (*no answer*) Afraid I'd look around at the pines and the brook and say, "Here? *Live?!*" (*Both laugh at her mugging of her own attitude.*) And the worst of it is you'd be right. I would say exactly that. (*dropping her head a bit*) I'm sorry, Sid. Your mountain girl has turned into an urban wastelander. I feel like watching television. I feel like sitting in a stupid movie—or even a nightclub, a real stupid nightclub with dirty jokes and bad dancers and—

SIDNEY. (*He shakes his head as if to wish what she is saying away.*) Iris, listen! Listen to the woods. Let's go for a walk.

IRIS. (*huddling close*) It's too cold. And dark. And the woods frighten me.

SIDNEY. All right then, let's go into the cabin and I'll make us a bang-up fire and some of the hottest coffee ever brewed— (*She just looks at him.*) You just want to go back to the city, don't you?

IRIS. Yes.

SIDNEY. You really hate it here?

IRIS. Yes. (*quietly*) Sid, I was born in country like this, the real thing. I mean you didn't drive out somewhere to *see* it. You just sat down on the back porch and there it was. Something to run from, to get the hell away from as fast as you could. When I got off that train from Trenersville I sure knew one thing: I wanted things—a life—men—as different from Oklahoma and—and Papa as possible. Papa was so crude and stupid . . . You know, I never heard my father make an abstract thought in his life, and, well, he had plenty of time to think, if you know what I mean. Didn't work that steady. And each of us, I think we've sort of grown up wanting some part of Papa that we thought was missing in him. I wanted somebody who could, well, think. Mavis wanted somebody steady and ordinary. And Gloria, well, you know —rich men. (*lifting her hand anticipating*) I know you're going to say that's parlor analysis, and it is, but—

SIDNEY. No, Iris. I'm listening. I really am. I am listening to you.

IRIS. And now something is happening, changing me. Sidney, I am 29 and I want to know that when I die more than ten or a hundred people will know the difference. I want to *make* it, Sid. Whatever that means and however it means it: that's what I want. (*He is nodding; for the moment, he genuinely understands.*) Anyhow, what does it do for you, Sid? To come up here and talk to your—your—?

SIDNEY. (*smiling*) My trolls.

IRIS. Yeah. Trolls. 'Cause I tried having a few words with 'em, and like what they had to say to me was nothing.

SIDNEY. (*looking around*) Coming here makes me believe the planet is mine again. In the primeval sense. That we have just been born, the earth and me, and are just starting out. There is no pollution, no hurt; just me and this ball of minerals and gasses suddenly shot together out of the cosmos. . . .

IRIS. (*looking at him, head tilted puppy-style, mouth ajar*) Jeees. (*They are quiet; he leans over and kisses her gently and at last, as she reciprocates fully, passionately.*) Oh, Sidney, Sidney . . .

SIDNEY. I love you very much.

IRIS. (*taking his hand meaningfully*) Take me into the cabin. (*He picks her up and they start in—but abruptly the clatter of GARBAGE CANS and the grinding roar of a GARBAGE TRUCK are heard and, simultaneously, reality—the LAMP and bedroom LIGHT—come up.)* Oh, shit, Sidney! Your *trolls* are here for the garbage—(*looks at her watch*) and your nymph is due at the pancake house in twenty minutes! (*ruffles his hair*) Take a shower, Mountain Man!

BLACKOUT

SCENE 2

TIME: *An evening in late summer. In the dark a SOUND-TRUCK blares out the buoyant, boisterous strains of* "The Wally O'Hara Campaign Song,"* *sung by a folk group with CROWD joining in on the chant and chorus.*

AT RISE: *As the soundtruck moves off, SIDNEY, WALLY, ALTON and MAX enter* D.L. *and across, singing, carrying flag, picket signs and a batch of leaflets. The signs read:* "O'Hara for Fair Housing/ Jobs/ Education," "Save the 20¢ Subway Fare," "End Police Brutality," "You *Can* Fight City Hall," *and—below the Picasso peace dove—*"Ban the Bomb." *(They are not picketing with these, merely bringing them home, and there may be more signs, including duplicates.)*

ALL. (*singing, clowning, harmonizing*)
"Sing out the old, sing in the new
It's your ballot and it's got a lot of work to do;

---

*See p. 134.

Sweep out the old, sweep in the new
Wally O'Hara is the man for you!

Wally O'Hara, Wally O'Hara,
Wally O'Hara is the man for you!"

WALLY. I tell you, boyos, something's happening! We're not just going to scare the bastards. We are going to beat them! (*SIDNEY, ALTON and MAX look at each other blankly.*)

ALTON. Did you hear the man?

MAX. I heard him.

WALLY. I mean it, fellas.

ALTON. (*feeling WALLY's forehead*) He's sick.

MAX. What's the matter with him?

SIDNEY. (*takes pulse; shakes his head*) All the symptoms. (*gravely*) Campaign Syndrome—the V.D. of the Body Politic. It always starts with delusions.

ALTON. (*nods*) The Dementia of the Dark Horse.

SIDNEY. And from there it spreads to the vital organs.

ALTON. Candidatitis Interruptus.

SIDNEY. Infantile Analysis.

MAX. Coalition Hemorrhoids.

ALTON. Is there nothing can save him?

SIDNEY. Nothing.

SIDNEY, ALTON & MAX. He really thinks he is going to win!

WALLY. Gentlemen, I thank you. And I leave you with the memorable words of the doubting public to Wilbur and Orville Wright: (*hands outstretched, oracularly*) "If God had intended men to fly, He would have given them—credit cards!" (*in brogue, high kick*) Tahmarrah O'Hara! C'mon, fellas. (*He leads MAX and ALTON off,* D.R., *almost bumping into DAVID, who is on the way to his apartment.*)

SIDNEY. David! Son of a gun. C'mon in and we'll drink to your first suh-mash hit! (*noting the newspapers which DAVID is carrying and trying to hide*) What'd you do, buy up every paper in the city!

DAVID. They're for my mother. That sort of thing matters to her . . . (*SIDNEY opens the door and he and DAVID carry the flag and the signs in, which they lean against the bookcase.*)

SIDNEY. Iris! Iris, where are you? IRIS—

IRIS. (O.S. *in bathroom; with exaggerated restraint*) I am *trying* to take a bath! Sidney, did you tell Alton it was all right to leave the loudspeaker in the *bathtub*?

SIDNEY. (*surprised innocence*) Who me? That clown! (*He goes outside for the leaflets. PHONE rings. He gets it.*) No, no, no . . . (*consulting tacked-up wall map of the Village*) You're in the Eighth Election District.

IRIS. (O.S.) And *who* gave this number as the canvassing headquarters?!

SIDNEY. No, it's not a mistake: Fourth Street *does* cross Eleventh Street. (*hangs up*)

IRIS. (O.S.) Sid-nee, I haven't been off the phone all—

SIDNEY. Don't worry, Iris. It's just until—

IRIS. (O.S.) Until *what*, darling-pie?

SIDNEY. (*PHONE rings. He gets it.*) Yes, Evie . . . The Knights of Columbus? . . . Well, *sure* O'Hara's Italian! (*hangs up, shrugs, to DAVID*) Well, his mother *could* be . . .

IRIS. (O.S.) *Until what*, Sid-nee?

SIDNEY. (*changing the subject*) Hey, did you see the reviews, honey? We don't have to put on anymore. We *know* a celebrity.

DAVID. Will you cut it out.

SIDNEY. Just listen. (*Snatching up a newspaper, he reads aloud.*) ". . . Mr. Ragin has found a device which transcends language itself. In his inspired 'Refrigerator,' all façade fades, all panaceas dissolve, and the ultimate questions are finally asked of existence itself . . ." (*the obvious joke on himself*) See. Just like I always said. (*looking about*) Oh, Iris, where'd Max leave the mailing piece?

IRIS. (*opens bathroom, wrapped in a towel*) Where *else*, Sid-nee? On top of the glasses!! (*She almost bumps into the flag.*) And if you don't get that junk out of here, I am going to *burn* the apartment down!!! *Asto diabolo! K'esi ki ehgloyes sou!** (*Exits into bedroom with a string of Greek expletives; SIDNEY finds stack of mailing pieces and box of envelopes, stacks them on coffee table and, whistling the Campaign Song, begins stuffing.*)

DAVID. (*studying him as a specimen*) I take it you really believe there is something to be achieved by all this?

SIDNEY. (*not taking the bait; gaily:*) C'mon, David. There is work to be done. Lend a hand.

DAVID. (*joining him at envelopes*) Well, I don't attack you for it. Hope is something most men, even thinking men, cling to long after they know better.

SIDNEY. (*between envelopes, not even raising his eyes*) Ah, you mean it is all an illusion! Zarathustra has spoken and God is dead? (*DAVID nods.*) "Progress" is a pipedream and the only reality is—nothing.

DAVID. Can one debate it?

SIDNEY. (*Finally sitting back for this: he feels himself in fine fettle, ready to take on anything. With rollicking flippancy:*) One can observe that it is the *debate* which is beside the point! The *debate* which is absurd, my boy!

---

* Pronounced: Ah-stoh' dee-yah' boh-loh. Keh-see' ghee eh gloh-yess' soo.

The "why" of why we are here is an intrigue for adolescents. The "how" is what command the living. Which is why— (*with a flourish*) I have lately become an insurgent again! (*PHONE rings. He gets it, sobers immediately.*) Yes, this is he. Mr. Dafoe . . . Oh? Oh . . . I see, sir. But we've already set the ad series in print . . . Yes, but I'm expecting a large check . . . Can't we talk about—? (*slowly hangs up*)

DAVID. Trouble?

SIDNEY. Did I say it was *easy* to be an insurgent, David? (*then more soberly*) Nothing that a little contribution to the free press wouldn't solve . . . Say, three thou . . . (*He wanders to the window and stands looking out, weighing something.*)

IRIS. (*Enters wearing the dress MAVIS bought, high-heel pumps in hand; he does not see her.*) David! My God. It's marvelous. (*embraces him; reaching for the reviews*) Gimme, gimme, gimme . . .

DAVID. (*embarrassed by her display*) Iris, *please*. I'll pick them up later. Got to get to work. (*starts out*)

IRIS. "Work!?" Already? Aren't you going to bask awhile or something?

DAVID. Doing what? See you. (*exits upstairs*)

SIDNEY. (*at the window*) Say, Iris, what did Mavis say about Fred's new promotion, the Folk River Dam thing? Y'know, I think maybe that solid old brother-in-law of mine might just be the man to— (*turns and sees the dress*) Well, get you!

IRIS. (*pirouettes*) I look pretty all right in this—huh, Sid?

SIDNEY. Sure, if you like the type. I like you in other things better.

IRIS. I know. I'm—going out tonight, Sidney.

SIDNEY. (*His mind is elsewhere.*) Yeah? Where? Sure,

sure, maybe I'll just call old Fred. (*catching himself*) Where, honey?

IRIS. I talked to Lucille Terry today. She's having a cocktail party.

SIDNEY. *Lucille Terry!?* Where in the name of God did she pop up from?

IRIS. Well, you know, just like that people suddenly call each other up. So just like that she called me up about this party she's having.

SIDNEY. Great. (*crosses to the phone*)

IRIS. (*in a muted voice*) Lucy didn't call me, Sid. I called her.

SIDNEY. How about that! You know something, Iris? Since we came out for Wally, almost a third of our advertisers have cancelled ads.

IRIS. (*At the moment she couldn't care less.*) Oh, really . . .

SIDNEY. (*starts to dial, then hangs up*) Fix me a drink, why doncha, honey? (*She hears, but does not oblige. He picks up the receiver, depressing the button to prevent connection. Hypothetical pitch, with forced heartiness:*) Hello, Fred? Just a social call. HOW'RE YOU AND HOW'S MAVIS AND HOW'D YOU LIKE TO BAIL OUT A FAILING WEEKLY?? You wouldn't . . ." (*another tack, another voice*) Hello, Fred ol' buddy! You hardly recognize my voice? . . . The nightclub? Well, y'see there's this newspaper—Oh? You're late for an appointment. . . ." (*He shrugs, picks up receiver, starts to dial, slams it down.*) Who needs him! (*a beat*) *I* need him. (*dials, abruptly hangs up*) I'll call him tomorrow! (*noticing her standing there, just looking at him quietly*) Aw, I'm sorry, honey, but I just don't feel like a party tonight. Tell Lucy we love her but no.

IRIS. (*starkly*) I wasn't asking you to come with me, Sidney. (*He drinks, slowly absorbs this last remark and, for the first time reacts.*)

SIDNEY. Oh?

IRIS. That's sort of the point. I—I am going alone. (*They are both quiet, neither looking at the other; the awkwardness shouts.*)

SIDNEY. Well, hell—Great. You should do things alone sometimes. Everybody should. What are we acting so funny about it for?

IRIS. Because we know it isn't just *a* party. It's the fact that I want to go. That *I* called Lucy. (*She looks at him—hurting for him.*) I'm sorry, Sid.

SIDNEY. (*turns to face her finally*) Who's going to be at this party, Iris?

IRIS. How do I know who's going to be there? Lucy's friends.

SIDNEY. The "would-be" set, as I recall it.

IRIS. Some of her friends are pretty successful.

SIDNEY. *Like Ben Asch?* (*She wheels and they exchange a violent conversation without words.*)

IRIS. (*getting into her shoes*) Look, Sid, let's make an agreement based on the recognition of reality. The reality being: the big thaw has set in with us and we don't know what that means yet. So until we do—well—let's not ask each other a whole lot of slimy questions.

SIDNEY. I'll ask all the slimy questions I want! Listen, Iris, have you been seeing this clown?

IRIS. Only once—after the time I told you.

SIDNEY. Once is all it takes.

IRIS. He thinks he can help me.

SIDNEY. Do what?

IRIS. Break in, that's what!

SIDNEY. Then why didn't he see *us*?

IRIS. I don't know, Sidney, I guess he was under the impression that I was a big girl now.

SIDNEY. I'll bet!

IRIS. Ben knows some extremely influential people. People who *do* things they mean to do.

SIDNEY. Where?

IRIS. In the theatre and in politics too! Especially in politics. People who do not take on a newspaper they cannot even afford and practically throw it away on a hopeless campaign. And for what? For Wally? If even half of what they say about Wally is true—

SIDNEY. Oh? And just what do "they" say? (*He waits, knowing there is nothing she can say.*)

IRIS. (*stubbornly*) Well, I don't know about any of this, but Lucy says they own Wally—

SIDNEY. (*Holding up one hand; the issue is closed.*) Right the first time, Iris! You don't know.

IRIS. Sidney, this is not Walden Pond. These people are sharks.

SIDNEY. (*With deliberate finality; father knows best.*) Look, Iris, I'll make a deal with you: you let me fight City Hall and I'll stay out of Shubert Alley.

IRIS. (*looking him in the eyes*) That's the way you want it?

SIDNEY. That's the way I want it.

IRIS. (*Quietly; she has had it.*) All right, Sidney. (*She starts out.*)

SIDNEY. And stop ducking the main point. What is this glorious doer Ben Asch going to do for you?

IRIS. As a matter of fact he's already got me some work.

SIDNEY. Oh? What show?

IRIS. It isn't exactly a show—but it *is* acting. Sort of . . . It's a TV commercial . . .

SIDNEY. (*laughing*) Oh, Iris, Iris.

IRIS. (*hotly, flinging bag down on couch*) Oh, aren't we better than everybody, Sidney Brustein! Well, I have news: it beats hell out of slinging hash while I wait for "pure art" to come along!

SIDNEY. Iris—

IRIS. And studying with every has-been actor who's teaching now because he can't work anymore!

SIDNEY. From the has-beens to the would-be's, I'll admit there's a progression there! Iris, it's not just what you're getting into—it's *how*. How can it be after five years of life with me that you don't know better than this? (*He has taken hold of her.*)

IRIS. (*exploding, near tears*) I have learned *a lot* after five years of life with you, Sidney Brustein! When I met you I thought Kant was a stilted way of saying cannot. I thought Puccini was a kind of spaghetti. I thought the louder an actor yelled and fell on the floor the greater he was. But you taught me to look deeper and harder. At everything. From Japanese painting to acting. Including Sidney, my *own* acting. Thanks to you, I now know something I wouldn't have without you. The fact—the *fact* that I am probably the world's *lousiest* actress . . . (*He releases her.*) So, there it is, the trouble with looking at ourselves honestly, Sidney, is that we come up with the truth. And, baby, the truth is a bitch! (*IRIS goes out the door.*)

SIDNEY. (*going after her*) Iris, Iris, just listen—

IRIS. (*Facing him; resolutely; she will not be stopped.*) All I know is that, from now on, I just want something to happen in my life. I don't much care *what*. Just something.

SIDNEY. I just want you to know that—whatever happens—you've been one of the few things in my life that made me happy.

IRIS. (*an anguished voice—for both of them*) Oh, Sid, "happy." (*She reaches up gently to touch his face.*) Who-ever started that anyhow? What little bastard was it? Teaching little kids there was such a thing. (*She exits,* D.R. *SIDNEY goes back inside, sits, goes to the drawing board, leaves that, picks up his banjo and then, with resolution, throws open the door.*)

SIDNEY. Hey—David . . . David! Can you come down a sec— (*But DAVID is right there, on his way out, in trenchcoat.*)

DAVID. (*a grin*) Oh, you caught me. Waaaal, I decided to go out after all. It—it seemed emptier than usual up there. I swore I wouldn't, you know— (*embarrassed*) sort of go out and strut around . . . But by God, it's al-most like I *have* to. I mean— (*He laughs freely and drops his hands.*) I *feel pretty good.*

SIDNEY. (*half steering, half pushing him inside*) Well, why not! Who wouldn't? . . . C'mon in a sec . . .

DAVID. Don't make fun of me, Sidney! The truth is today is not yesterday. Nothing could have made me be-lieve this yesterday, but—I am somebody else today. It's in my rooms, it's in my coat . . . it's in my skin. Christ, Sid— (*pure unadulterated wonder; donning the chic shades he has been carrying*) *I'm famous.* (*embraces him; then:*) I have to go out and find out what it's like to wear it in the streets. (*sobering*) As if I can't guess. Everybody will just be more self-conscious, phonier than yesterday. Just because my picture was in the pa-pers. It's crazy. The phone keeps on ringing. For years I made fun of people who had unlisted numbers. First thing Monday—I get one. (*final smile*) G'night, Sid.

SIDNEY. No, wait a minute. Please. I'd like to talk to you. You want a drink? (*crosses to bar*)

DAVID. (*sits impatiently*) What do you want, Sidney? I'm in a hurry.

SIDNEY. (*not looking at him, as he mixes drinks*) Hey —David . . . it's as good as on, isn't it?

DAVID. What—?

SIDNEY. (*a little madly*) Your next play. Every producer in town will be—

DAVID. (*annoyed to talk about this; a modest person*) Well . . . my agent said there've been some calls . . . (*a sigh about producers*) First you can't get into their offices, then you can't get out of them—

SIDNEY. (*advancing, drinks in hand*) You're very talented, David.

DAVID. I have to go.

SIDNEY. No. (*DAVID sinks back.*) Look, remember that play that Iris was in a couple of years ago?

DAVID. Yes?

SIDNEY. Well, you thought she was pretty good. Even better than I did . . . You said so.

DAVID. Those were my polite years. When I still cared what people thought about me.

SIDNEY. No, come on, you said she was pretty good.

DAVID. When she just danced. When she spoke, when she had lines— (*shrugs helplessly*) it was horrible.

SIDNEY. Well, not *horrible*. Just average.

DAVID. What do you want, Sidney? (*He rises.*)

SIDNEY. She's a hung-up kid, David. She needs something to happen for her.

DAVID. (*unrelentingly*) What is it that you want, Sidney?

SIDNEY. Write her into your play, David. Something simple. With dancing maybe.

DAVID. (*absorbing it*) I have to go now, Sid.

SIDNEY. It wouldn't have to be a big part, for Christ's sake! Look, she *needs* something to happen for her, don't you understand?

DAVID. You solve your marriage problems any way you have to, Sidney. I won't judge you. But don't bring them to me. (*He opens the door.*)

SIDNEY. (*suddenly blurting*) I'll do the review— (*SIDNEY stops himself, amazed at the thought.*)

DAVID. (*turning slowly back to him*) What did you say? (*SIDNEY is quiet, knowing the enormity of his error.*) Okay, Sid, I'll pretend I never heard you. I am going out now. I don't need to experience the other part of this scene. The Recovery of Morality and all that. That's *uptown* drama. I can't stand those. (*He starts out again, fast. SIDNEY grabs him.*)

SIDNEY. What's so awful about it? For Christ's sake, can't you write about more than two characters at a time?

DAVID. (*removing SIDNEY's hands*) Sidney, I'll tell you something. Prostitutes interest me clinically; I've not the least intention of ever becoming one.

SIDNEY. (*in profound humiliation*) Don't feel so holy about it, David. I asked and you refused. Let's forget it. It was such a little—such a tiny little act on the part of a slightly desperate man. . . .

DAVID. Such a tiny little corruption. That's the magic of the tiny corruptions, isn't it? Their insignificance makes them so appealing.

SIDNEY. (*crossing away*) I said let's forget it.

DAVID. No, let's not. (*lifting his glass sardonically*) The fact is I should thank you. I was really too mellow to go out in this world. Too vulnerable. I would have been torn to pieces. (*toasts*) I'm ready for it now. (*He drinks and turns to go—as WALLY enters* D.R., *in high jubilance, doing minstrel kicks, wiggling hat above* *head, and singing a few bars of a song like "When the Red, Red Robin Comes Bob, Bob, Bobbin' Along."* Dryly:*) Enter, the future.

WALLY. Could be, could be. Allow me to offer the grim Past a leaflet. (*crossing to SIDNEY*) Sidney, you should have seen the crowd on Bleecker Street. Remember, boyo, you heard it from O'Hara first: we are going to *win* this thing!

DAVID. (*crumpling the leaflet*) You know, it is my fondest hope and greatest expectation that one of these days the hoods will just get tired of you children and wrap you up in sacks and drop you in the river as in the old days. (*He lets it fall, turns and exits.*)

WALLY. (*limp-wristedly, mocking him*) "Well, I hope yew got that!"

SIDNEY. (*offended*) Wally, cut it out! I don't like that. (*troubled*) Besides, David has the nasty habit of sometimes being right. (*sits heavily in rocker*)

WALLY. Ah me, ah me: pessimism is weighing heavily on the land. (*a beat; studying SIDNEY*) How's Iris?

SIDNEY. Fine.

WALLY. She seems to be spending a lot of time lately with the girl friend of one of my poker-playing buddies.

SIDNEY. If you were married, you'd understand.

WALLY. Seems like a funny crowd for Iris. (*realizing that SIDNEY is doubled over with pain*) What's the matter?

SIDNEY. My ulcer is having a rock-and-roll party.

WALLY. Where's your medicine?

---

*Caution:** permission to produce *The Sign in Sidney Brustein's Window* does *not* include permission to use this song in production. Producers should procure these rights from the copyright owner of the song.

SIDNEY. In the bathroom. The brown bottle. (*bitterly*) They're tranquilizers.

WALLY. (*goes in; reading from the bottle*) Says you're supposed to take one every morning. Didn't you take it?

SIDNEY. No.

WALLY. Why not?

SIDNEY. Because I hate them.

WALLY. Don't be such a nut. They keep you from getting upset about every little thing. (*He hands the pills to SIDNEY.*)

SIDNEY. (*turning his head slowly to his friend*) "Every little thing," huh, Wally? Yes, by all means hand me the chloroform of my passions; the sweetening of my conscience; the balm of my glands. (*lifting the pills like Poor Yorick's skull*) Oh blessèd age! — that has provided that I need never live again in the full temper of my rage! (*Rising and crossing to drawing board, he picks up a yardstick, which, in his hand, becomes the "sword" of the speech.*) In the ancient times, the good men among my ancestors, when they heard of evil, strapped a sword to their loins and strode into the desert. And when they found it — (*He "draws" and measures the enemy.*) *they cut it down*! (*He slashes away.*) Or were cut down and bloodied the earth with purifying death. (*Looking up at "the sword" he remembers himself: the hand falls and with it the bearing of the man.*) But how does one confront these thousand nameless faceless vapors that are the evil of our time? Could a *sword* pierce it? . . . Look at me, Wally! . . . *Wrath* — (*The word should ring with Biblical righteous indignation.*) has become a poisoned gastric juice in the intestine. One does not *smite* evil anymore: one holds one's gut, thus — and takes a pill. (*as he rises suddenly to full Jovian stance*) Oh, but to take up the sword of the Maccabees again! (*He closes down from the mighty gesture and sets down the "sword," then lamely takes his pill and water.) L'chaim!*

DIMOUT

SCENE 3

TIME: *Primary night. Early September. In the darkness the sounds of a not-too distant victory celebration: SHOUTING, CHEERS and JUBILATION, the indistinct mumble of a LOUDSPEAKER, snatches of the Campaign Song, sung and chanted by the CROWD.*

AT RISE: *SIDNEY and MAX enter,* U.R., *singing and cavorting, as high on victory as drink. Once in the door they head for the bar.*

SIDNEY & MAX. (*from* My Fair Lady)
"I said to him, we did it!
We did it! We did it!
I said that we could do it
And indeed we did!

SIDNEY.
Tonight, old man, you did it!

MAX.
You did it! You did it!—"

(*They raise their glasses.*)

SIDNEY. It was nothing, Mr. Gallagher!

MAX. You're too modest, Mr. Sheean! (*They clink glasses and drink.*)

SIDNEY. Can you believe it, Max? (*Sudden inspiration as he recalls a McGuffey's Reader-type poem. He strikes a pose, then tramps gleefully about the stage to the exag-*

gerated beat of the lines. The rapid-fire delivery should not exceed fifteen seconds.)

"Somebody said that it couldn't be done,
But he with a chuckle replied—
That MAYBE IT COULDN'T, but he would be one
Who wouldn't say No 'til he tried.
So he buckled right in, with the trace of a grin
On his face—if he worried, he hid it.
He started to sing, as he tackled the thing
That couldn't be done, AND HE DID IT!"

(*on one knee, arms outstretched*) Ta da! (*sudden thought*) David! Where's that David? (*goes outside*) Where is that sad-eyed little bastard today? Twenty years of political history overturned and he goes into hiding! Hey, STRINDBERG! Strindberg, WHERE ARE YOU? What are you avoiding the partisans for today, huh?

IRIS. (*at bedroom door, in robe, hair up in towel*) Sssshhh, Sidney! I'm trying to sleep.

SIDNEY. You're not Strindberg! Thank God you're not Strindberg. You're not even Ibsen! (*He reaches to embrace her, she disengages and he reels back to door.*) Hey, KIERKEGAARD!

IRIS. Leave him alone.

SIDNEY. Leave him alone, hell! I'm going to make that sophomoric little elf eat his pessimistic profundities with a spoon. (*His eye catches MAX, who is about to leave.*) Hey, Max! You know the trouble with us believers in this world?

MAX & SIDNEY. (*old refrain*) "We don't *believe*!"

SIDNEY. You wanna know a secret, Max? Scout's honor? (*MAX shakes his head.*) Even *I* didn't believe it! That it could happen! That— (*savouring the words*) college kids and little old ladies and taxidrivers and skinny little Madison Avenue ad men—wops and kikes and micks and niggers and WASPS, eggheads, faggots, kooks, you name it—would all get up one day and go out and wipe out the Boss! *Zap!* Can you believe it?

MAX. (*ponders this a second, then:*) Sure, why not? (*looks at his watch*) Oh, Jesus, she'll castrate me! (*He exits,* D.R.)

SIDNEY. (*still with wonder, with awe*) Iris. Do you *realize* what we proved today?

IRIS. (*with a weary half-smile*) No, Sidney, what did you prove?

SIDNEY. That what the people want is alternatives, that's all! Give them real alternatives and all the dull, stupid old shibboleths go up in smoke! *Poof!* We don't know a goddamn thing about the human race!

IRIS. (*Shakes her head; SIDNEY does not catch the undercurrent.*) Sidney, I'm exhausted . . . I've got to get some—

SIDNEY. (*Possessed; he can see it* all.) In a minute, baby. Sit down. Sit down. Just listen to little old Sidney. (*He plops her down on the couch. All exuberance: a steamroller going downhill.*) Iris, do you know how *old* the world is?

IRIS. Sidney—

SIDNEY. Why the whole fucking planetary system is only five billion years old. And it was only 25 *million* years ago that primitive apes were strolling around at half-stoop—by eternity's measures maybe one day and one night! (*She sighs, starts to get up. Rapidly.*) And they were apes, honey. Not *men*. APES! Do you get me, Iris? By God, this is beautiful! (*She looks at him blankly, very polite.*) And then—finally—a long, *long* time after that: Cro-Magnon Man! A mere, lousy nothing of a teensie little thirty thousand years ago—Iris, *he's a baby*! He's an infant!

IRIS. (*wearily*) Who, Sid?

SIDNEY. *Man! The human race!* (*He flops down beside her, spent but gratified.*) Yesterday he made a wheel and fire and—and figured out a calendar and how to make the corn grow—and today we're writing him off because he hasn't made universal beauty and wisdom and truth, too! (*lifting his eyes to hers with a plaintive joy*) All he needs is a little more time and he'll be all right, doncha think, honey? Time and alternatives, like today? (*She says nothing.*) . . . Iris?

IRIS. (*finally, simply*) Sidney, I took the sublet. (*He sobers immediately; a beat.*)

SIDNEY. (*desperately trying to maintain his cool*) Hot and cold running electricity?—When?

IRIS. (*averting her eyes*) Monday.

SIDNEY. (*foolishly*) Monday.

IRIS. (*She nods; a beat.*) Well. You did a terrific job, Sid. Congratulations.

SIDNEY. (*with more than a trace of irony*) Thanks.

IRIS. (*Brightening; cheerily, to break the mood*) Hey, congratulate *me.* It's a big night for me, too, remember? (*He stares at her.*) I do my first commercial—did I tell you they rented the Four Seasons after hours? (*He looks away with discomfort. The smile fades on her face.*) Never mind, it's not important. "Would-be" stuff, right? Just little old "would-be" Iris. *Wo*man—not the human race! (*gets up and starts towards the bedroom*)

SIDNEY. No, Iris, it *is* important. I don't think that at all. If it's what you want—

IRIS. (*to end this*) Sidney, I'm tired and I'm scared about tonight. I've *got* to try and get a little sleep. (*hesitates in the doorway*) I'll get my stuff out as soon as I . . .

SIDNEY. (*as bravely as he can manage it*) Hey. It's still your bedroom—until you turn into a pumpkin . . .

IRIS. (*helplessly*) Oh, Sid. (*She goes to him, kisses his

head consolingly. During this ALTON has entered D.R. *He knocks agitatedly, knocks again, opens the door. IRIS makes a quick recovery; too cheerily:*) Hi, Alt. Hey, Gloria breezed into town this morning. She's been trying to get you. (*singing and mugging*)

"She didn't say yes, she didn't say no . . ."

(*ALTON is grimly silent.*) Anyhow, she'll be by later. (*waving gaily*) *Ciao.* (*disappears into bedroom, then pops her head out*) And, Sid, please: even if *all* the Kennedy's show up for your endorsement, I'm *not* here! Okay? (*exits*)

SIDNEY. (*stands looking after her, at last rouses himself*) Hey, Alton—can you *believe* it?

"I said to him, We did it!
We did it—"

In a million years I didn't believe— (*noticing his expression at last*) Say, were you pulling for the other side or something? What's with you, man? You don't show up at the polls—you skip the victory rally—

ALTON. Is it true, Sid?

SIDNEY. (*knowing at once*) Is what true—?

ALTON. C'mon, Sid, we've hung out a long time, don't crap around. Is it *true*? Is it true she's a hooker? (*They stare at each other a long moment, then:*) And you were going to let me marry her . . . ? (*SIDNEY exhales a great sigh and sits.*) Why didn't you tell me?

SIDNEY. It wasn't my place. It was for Gloria to tell you. She loves you, Alt. (*ALTON bursts into laughter.*) Look, I thought you'd be man enough to help Gloria—like you want to help the rest of the world—

ALTON. Talk to me man to man today, Sidney: would you marry her?

SIDNEY. Alton, for Christ's sake! You call yourself a revolutionary! Doesn't that stand for anything anymore!

ALTON. (*unrelenting*) Would you marry her?

SIDNEY. (*shouting*) Is it one thing to take bread to the Bowery and another to eat it with them?

ALTON. *Would you marry her?*

SIDNEY. If I loved her . . . If you love a woman, Alton . . . Look, don't do it, man. Not today. Just don't make me sick today. Just don't act like a fraternity boy meeting his own girl under the lamppost. (*He rises and crosses quickly into the bathroom for his pills.*)

ALTON. When you go into the mines, Sid, you get coal in your skin. If you're a fisherman, you reek of fish. She doesn't *know* how to love anymore. It's all a performance!

SIDNEY. You're wrong, Alt, she—

ALTON. Don't you know some of the things these girls have to do!

SIDNEY. All right, I know. I know. You are afire with all the images: every faceless man in the universe has become—

ALTON. (*looking off*) Someone who has coupled with my love . . . used her . . . like a thing, man . . . an instrument . . . a commodity . . .

SIDNEY. People change, Alt. She'll change. She needs someone. (*with his own thoughts*) Everyone needs someone . . .

ALTON. *THE WHITE MAN DONE WRAPPED HIS TRASH IN TINSEL AND GIVE IT TO THE NIGGER AGAIN, HUH, SIDNEY?!* . . . Don't you understand, man? Like I am SPAWNED from commodities—and their purchasers! Don't you *know* this? How do you think I got the color I am? I got this color from my grandmother being used as a commodity, man! The buying and the selling in this country began with *me*, Jesus help me! (*It is not a cry for help, but a shriek of pain against the universe.*)

SIDNEY. All right.

ALTON. (*smiling bitterly to himself*) You don't understand . . . My father, you know, he was a railroad porter . . . who wiped up spit and semen, carried drinks and white man's secrets for thirty years. When the bell rang in the night he put on that white coat and his smile and went shuffling through the corridors with his tray and his whisk broom, his paper bags and his smile . . . to wherever the white men were ringing . . . for *thirty years*! And my mother, she was a domestic. She always had, Mama did, bits of this and bits of that from the pantry of "Miss Lady," you know. Some given, some stolen . . . And she would always bring this booty home and sit it all out on the kitchen table . . . so's we could all look at it. And my father—all the time he would stand there and look at it and walk away. And then one night— (*He is reliving the scene.*) he had some kind of fit, and he just reached out and knocked all that stuff—the jelly and the piece of ham, the broken lamp and the sweater for me—he just knocked it all on the floor and stood there screaming with the tears running down his face: "I ain't going to have the white man's leavings in my house, no mo'! I AIN'T GOING TO HAVE HIS *THROW-AWAY* . . . NO MO'!" . . . And Mama, she just stood there with her lips pursed together, and when he went to bed she just picked it all up, whatever hadn't been ruined or smashed, and washed it off and brushed it off and put it in the closet . . . and we *ate* it and we *used* it because we had to *survive*, and she didn't have room for my father's pride . . . (*a beat*) I don't want white man's leavings, Sidney. Not now. Not ever. (*taking out an envelope*) I wrote her a note. (*without looking at him, hands it to SIDNEY—who does not take it*)

SIDNEY. Aren't you even going to see her? (*ALTON*

shakes his head quickly.) Are you afraid you'd forgive her? (*ALTON drops the note on the table and starts out.*) And if she were *black*? (*ALTON halts, but does not face him.*) At least you'd see her . . .

ALTON. *You* see her—!

SIDNEY. That's *racism*, Alt!

ALTON. (*turning in the door*) Don't give me that shit! Oppression is not equal and you know it!

SIDNEY. I know that Gloria is no more a commodity than your grandmother—she's a human being, Alt! A *victim*!

ALTON. (*evenly*) Yeah, well, like, my grandmother *never* had her options! (*He crosses out and* D.R.)

SIDNEY. (*shouting after him from the door*) And what about *you*? No choices for you either—is that what it comes to, Alt? (*crossing towards him to give back the envelope*) At least *see* her, man. Give her that much.

ALTON. (*anguished, torn; a beat*) I can't, Sidney.

SIDNEY. Why not?

ALTON. Because—Oh, man, like I know it all here—(*touches his forehead*) but . . .

SIDNEY. (*ironically, finishing it for him*) —but this is not the hour, is it? "A star has risen over Africa—"

ALTON. (*vehemently*) Yes!

SIDNEY. Over Harlem . . .

ALTON. Right!

SIDNEY. Over the Southside . . .

ALTON. You got it!

SIDNEY. The New Zionism is raging. A flame consuming the soul! And nothing is larger—not love, not compassion . . . . Nothing???

ALTON. If that's the way you read it, baby—*noth-ing*! (*He exits across* D.L. *SIDNEY stands looking after him and at the envelope. He goes back in, pours himself a drink. There is a knock. He brightens and goes for it.*)

SIDNEY. Alt— (*As he opens it, MAVIS, who has entered* D.R., *bursts in arms outstretched with elation.*)

MAVIS. Sidney Brustein! Who'd of ever thought it! Fred's so excited he called me from the office: "Mav, that brother-in-law of yours is some kind of political genius!" Why, he said that everybody is talking about you and the paper and Wally O'Hara. It even went out on the national news. (*She has hugged and kissed him through most of this.*) Let's have a drink together, Sidney. I don't know how to tell you how proud I am. I just thought it was another one of those things you're always doing—like with the nightclub— (*correcting herself*) I know, it wasn't a nightclub—and all. Where is everyone? I thought this place would be—you know—

SIDNEY. (*fixing her a drink*) —"jumping"? I wasn't the candidate, Mav. Iris is exhausted. She had to turn in.

MAVIS. Turn in!? Aren't you kids going out and celebrate? Honest to God, you're so strange—you don't even look happy.

SIDNEY. Oh, I'm happy . . . Happy.

MAVIS. (*takes a check out of her bag and puts it in SIDNEY's shirt pocket*) Here's a little present, for the paper. (*noting his astonishment*) From *Fred*, let's say. No. Don't say a word.

SIDNEY. (*looking at it*) This is a lot of money, honey.

MAVIS. (*drinking*) Not a word! When I—that is when *Fred*—decided we agreed that we didn't want any chance whatsoever to feel good and gooey and Real Big about it. So—put it away. (*She takes out cigarettes and lighter and settles back.*)

SIDNEY. (*genuinely*) Well, thank you—Oh, I mean, *Fred*—for it.

MAVIS. (*warmly*) Shut up. (*the liquor warming and freeing her*) I'm glad to have a chance to talk with you, Sidney. Alone. (*He slumps back, feet crossed on coffee *table; resigned, but not really looking or listening.*) We've never really talked. I know that you don't like me—

SIDNEY. Mavis—

MAVIS. No, it's all right. I know it. You know it. When you come down to it, what is there to like? Isn't it funny how different sisters can be?

SIDNEY. Yes, different. All of us. Everything.

MAVIS. Yeeesss, don't I know it. I was trying to explain that to Fred the other day. (*a little laugh*) I don't mean "explain" it, that sounds so funny: Fred isn't a stupid man, as we all know— (*He nods vaguely from time to time.*) but sometimes. Sometimes I get to thinking that certain kind of way. The way, you know, that *you* do— (*with her hands, a circle, and aptly, the universe*) of a whole—?

SIDNEY. In abstractions.

MAVIS. That's right. You won't believe it—but—I enjoy it when a person can say something so that it embraces a lot, so that it's in—in—

SIDNEY. (*staring at her*) Concepts.

MAVIS. Yes. I enjoy it. I've enjoyed the conversations I've heard down here. And, Sidney, I've *understood* some of them. (*There is a curious, believable and quite charming defiance in this announcement.*)

SIDNEY. Good for you, Mavis. Good for you. (*gets up to refill glasses*)

MAVIS. (*oddly*) But we get stuck, you know.

SIDNEY. I know.

MAVIS. Some of us, we get stuck in— (*stiltedly*) the original stimuli. Some of us never have a chance, you know—

SIDNEY. (*nodding wearily as he sits and hands her drink*) I know—

MAVIS. Like Papa—he was such a dreamer. You know, sort of backwoods poet, kind of a cross between

Willy Loman and Daniel Boone. He loved just sitting and thinking—

SIDNEY. (*looking at her, stunned*) Mavis, didn't you and Iris have the same father?

MAVIS. Of course we had the same father! What do you think I'm talking about?

SIDNEY. (*throwing up his hands*) *Rashomon*—what else?!

MAVIS. He was a very wonderful man, very wonderful. And that's the joke on me—I thought I was marrying someone like Papa when I married Fred. Can you imagine—*Fred*!

SIDNEY. (*sitting upright*) You mean you *wanted* him to be like your father?

MAVIS. Yes . . . and that's the way I thought Fred was, in those days when we were courting. He *seemed* poetic. Like Papa. (*a little high*) Papa used to read the classics to us, you know, Greek tragedy. Sometimes in Greek.

SIDNEY. (*wide-eyed*) You're pulling my leg.

MAVIS. Why? Oh, he didn't really know *classical* Greek, Sidney. Just everyday Greek from his folks. We used to do little productions in our living room. He would always let me be Medea, because he said I was strong— (*She rises and bellows forth in robust, dramatic and effective* Greek *the following, enriching it with not badly conceived if stagey classical stance and gesture.*) 'Ο *πόνος μέ περικυκλώνει ἀπό ὄλες τίς μεριές καί ποιός μπορεῖ νά τό ἀμφισβητήση.* 'Αλλά *δέν χάθηκαν ἀκόμα ὄλα.* Ν*ομίζω ὄχι.** (*Then in English:*) "On all sides sorrow pens me in. But all is not yet lost! Think *not* so! Still

* Pronunciation: Uh puh-nuhss' meh peh-ree-keek-luh' nee ah-puh' hul' ess tees meh-ree-ess' keh pee-uhss buh-ree' nah tuh ahm-fee-vee-tee' see. Allah dehn kah' thee-kahn ah-kuhm' ah huh' lah. Nuh-mee' zuh uh' kee.

there are troubles in store for the new bride and for her bridegroom—" (*catching herself, a little embarrassed*) Well, *he* thought I was good.

SIDNEY. (*with wonder*) Mavis, I don't know you.

MAVIS. The ham part. (*a little laugh*) I know all the parts and all the strophes. Sure, Papa was something! He was a man of great, great imagination. That's why he changed our name. It was plain old every day Parapopadopoulos, you know—

SIDNEY. No, I didn't know.

MAVIS. But Papa wanted something, you know, *symbolic.* So he changed it to Parodus. You know what the parodus is in Greek tragedy. . . . (*She turns to him expectantly.*)

SIDNEY. (*nods "yes," then abruptly:*) . . . No.

MAVIS. (*proudly*) Sidney! Shame on you! The parodus is the chorus! And you know—no matter what is happening in the main action of the play—the chorus is always there, commenting, watching. Papa said that *we* were like that, the family, at the edge of life—not changing anything. Just watching and being.

SIDNEY. I see.

MAVIS. That was Papa, dramatic as hell. (*drinking her drink*) I loved him very much. (*a beat*) And Fred's no Papa.

SIDNEY. It's been one big disappointment, your marriage? (*He crosses to refill their glasses.*)

MAVIS. Not for a minute. By the time we got married I knew that Fred was no poet. Solid as a rock! Hah! (*abruptly*) We haven't touched each other more than twice since little Harry was born and that's . . . Harry will be six next month.

SIDNEY. Six years . . . Ah—by whose—

MAVIS. —design? Who knows? It just happens. (*A wave of her hand.*) He doesn't suffer. He's got a girl.

SIDNEY. (*wheeling, bottle in hand; gutturally:*) *Fred?*

MAVIS. *Fred.* You know, sometimes I think you kids down here believe your own notions of what the rest of the human race is like. There are no squares, Sidney. Believe me when I tell you, everybody is his own hipster. (*He digests this, turns back to pour her drink, then, on second thought, doubles it, raises it to her in a half toast, then crosses back and sits.*) Sure, for years now. Same girl, I'll say that for old Fred. I've met her.

SIDNEY. (*He would genuinely like to seem blasé but he can't; he is truly astonished.*) You have—?

MAVIS. (*all with ironic restraint*) Oh sure. He has her all set up. Nothing fancy; Fred's strictly a family man, he puts the main money in the main place, our Fred. But decent, you know, respectable building, family people —a nice place for a single girl— (*the ultimate bitterness*) with a kid. (*He absorbs this with a silent start but knows to say nothing.*) He's just a year younger than Harry. (*Now she is fighting tears. She fumbles at lighting a cigarette which SIDNEY finally does for her.*) Oh, you do find out. And so, one day, I did what a woman has to do: I went to see. Not the spooky thing. I didn't want to come in on them together or any of that junk. I know what a man and a woman do. I just wanted to see her. So I got in a cab, got out, rang a bell and there she was. Not a chorine or some cheap mess as you always think, but no, there's this sandy-haired kid in pedal pushers, pregnant as all get-out. So I said I rang the wrong bell. And I went back, once—to see the baby. In the park. I had to see the baby. And then, after that, the usual waltz . . . Divorce talk, all of it, you know.

SIDNEY. And you decided against it.

MAVIS. Of course I decided against it. A divorce? For what? Because a husband is unfaithful? Ha! We've got three boys and their father is devoted to them—I guess he's devoted to all four of his boys. And what would I do? There was no rush years ago to marry Mavis Parodus; there was *just* Fred then. In this world there are two kinds of loneliness: with a man and without one. I picked. And, let's face it, *I* cannot type.

SIDNEY. (*quietly shaking his head*) But you want only simple people and simple problems in literature . . .

MAVIS. Sure, isn't life enough? (*Long beat; setting glass down she rises and gathers her things: the moment is over.*) Well, one thing is sure. I do not need another drop to drink. (*fixing herself at bathroom mirror, compact in hand*) So how is my cream-colored brother-in-law-to-be?

SIDNEY. He's not going to be.

MAVIS. Well, thank God for something. She broke it off, huh?

SIDNEY. (*absorbing the assumption*) Yes . . . I guess so.

MAVIS. (*blithe ignorance again*) It had to be. Look, the world's not ready. It just isn't. (*He doesn't look at her. She crosses and sits next to him.*) I mean he seemed like a nice boy and all that, but it's just not possible. You have to think about children, you know. I mean he's very light, but— (*halting*) I'm not fooling you, am I?

SIDNEY. No.

MAVIS. I can't help it, Sid! It's the way I feel. You can't expect people to change that fast. (*She gets up to go.*)

SIDNEY. (*gently and almost off-handedly—more with sadness than assertion*) Mavis, the world is about to crack right down the middle. We've gotta change—or fall in the crack.

MAVIS. (*not angrily*) Well, I think we are back to ourselves and you are probably starting to insult me again. I knew I was going to tell you though, Sid, one of these days. Since I first saw you I knew those eyes could find a place for anybody's tale. Don't tell Iris though, huh?

She's a kid, Sidney. She'll get herself together one of these days. (*patting his cheek*) And so will you. (*looking at him*) Gee, we're proud of you, Sid. I told Fred, "Say what you will, but the Jews have get-up!"

SIDNEY. (*He winces—then, in that kind of mood:*) Say what you will.

MAVIS. Now, there was nothing wrong with that, was there?

SIDNEY. (*smiling*) Well, let's say there isn't. Today. (*A beat; she opens the door.*) Mavis, what do you do . . . I mean . . . ?

MAVIS. To make up for Fred, you mean? (*thoughtfully*) I take care of my boys. I shop. And I worry about my sisters. It's a life.

SIDNEY. (*a beat; gently, looking to the gods above; for their ears only*) "Witness you ever-burning lights above . . ." (*crosses to her*) You're tough, Mavis Parodus.

(*He kisses her. MAVIS, moved, touches his arm, and says nothing at all as she exits* D.R. *He stands for a moment, then goes back in, pours a drink and stands looking out his window at the celebration. IRIS peeks out of bedroom to make sure MAVIS is gone, and enters. She looks completely different: her hair yellow blonde, cut and teased and blown to perfection, clothes ultra-chic. She is all business. Determined at all costs, in the minutes remaining before she leaves, to avoid a scene and, above all, tears: to keep the conversation as light and bright and inconsequential as possible. She carries a smart shopping bag, which she sets on couch, and a large round vinyl hatbox. SIDNEY, at the window, does not see her.*)

IRIS. Thanks for covering. I couldn't have taken Mavis tonight.

SIDNEY. (*with his own thoughts*) It really wasn't such a—chore.

IRIS. What'd she bring me this time?

SIDNEY. (*with his newfound appreciation*) Love. Solicitude. (*He laughs.*) No. Actually, this time she brought *me* something. (*He turns, sees her, and rather freezes.*)

IRIS. I know. It looks pretty different. I won't ask you if you like it. (*SIDNEY says nothing. For once he is quiet. In a state of shock:*) It's for the job. They send you out to get fixed—pay for everything. (*A finger snap; she takes new shoes out of box in shopping bag. Putting them on:*) Even the shoes. (*She laughs.*) They say it's gauche to walk out of a store in shoes you've just bought. At least that's what poor people say. I guess nothing's gauche if you're rich enough. *Long* enough. (*straightening*) Please don't stare at me like that, Sid. (*She bends to smooth her stockings.*)

SIDNEY. (*with thoughtfulness*) Why did you always tell me all those stories about your father, Iris?

IRIS. (*looking up*) You and Mavis had yourselves a real little old heart-to-heart, didn't you? What's the world coming to?

SIDNEY. Why did you make him out to be some kind of dullwitted nothing?

IRIS. (*irritably, swiftly, falsely*) Oh, why do you believe Mavis? She has some kind of transference about Papa. (*She starts for bedroom.*) When she talks about Papa she's really talking about this uncle of ours who—

SIDNEY. (*knowing that she is going into a long involved lie*) Never mind, Iris. It doesn't matter.

IRIS. (*turning, her hand on knob; sincerely:*) I guess—I just tried to live up to your fantasy about me. All of it. People do that— (*She looks at him; exits into bedroom.*)

SIDNEY. (*calling after her*) She thought we'd be going out to celebrate. You haven't told her.

IRIS. (O.S.) No. Who wants to hear all the wailing?

SIDNEY. I have a hunch she'd survive it.

IRIS. (*re-enters with elegant coat or cape and brand new overnight bag and crosses to bathroom mirror for final touchup*) Mavis' idea of marriage is something you do at twenty and it stays that way no matter what. Everything else shocks. (*carefully positioning a curl*)

SIDNEY. Sure. Dullsville. (*Several beats; as he studies her and peers into shopping bag.*) By the way, Iris—what will you do? On the— (*gestures: "television"*) tube. I don't even know what it is you're actually— (*He holds this word for a fraction longer than ordinary meaning would dictate. She does not miss this and so signifies by a lift of brow.) selling.*

IRIS. (*evenly*) I am *selling* home permanents.

SIDNEY. Is that what—uh—they've used on you?

IRIS. (*determined not to let him provoke her*) Don't be funny. This head has been in and out of every booth in Mr. Lionel's!

SIDNEY. But that's *not* what you are going to tell the people, is it? That you got your— (*He reads from the label of a large golden elegant lettered box he has found in shopping bag.*) Golden Girl Curl at Mr. Lionel's?

IRIS. (*evenly, fighting for self-control*) No, Sid, that certainly is *not* what I am going to tell them. I am going— (*advancing on the sample box*) to tell all the little housewifies that I just rolled it up on Golden Girl Curl . . . (*Holding up the box, she assumes the manner and tone of TV mannequins, but just beneath the surface of her kidding is the edge of hysteria.*) and rollers, using my magic Golden Girl Curl Box to hold everything just so . . . which you understand, is one of the main features of Golden Girl Curl Home Permanent.

SIDNEY. The box it comes in.

IRIS. Yes! The box it comes in! (*She opens it—the bottom falls out** *and so do the rollers. Hurling it to the floor:*) Which also does not work!!! (*wheeling, crying, shrieking*) It's a job, Sidney! They do not pay you one hundred dollars an hour for serving pancakes! They do pay it for pretending that there is some difference between Golden Girl Curl and Wonder Curl, or between Wonder Curl and Home Perma Pearl, so what the hell do you want from me!

SIDNEY. It doesn't work . . .

IRIS. (*precisely now in the manner of a defensive child*) It *does* work! Enough. To justify it. They just send you to the hairdressers to play safe. They have to have everything just so when they tape things for television, Sidney. You don't realize how expensive it is—all those lights and cameras and technicians . . . they can't have your hair falling down from some . . . (*swiping at Golden Girl Curl again as her voice breaks in tears*) crappy old home permanent just when they're ready to SHOOT . . . !

SIDNEY. (*taking her in his arms*) What's the matter, baby, what's happening to you? What's it all about—?

IRIS. (*in his arms, sobbing*) Nothing . . . will put a curl in your hair . . . like this but . . . heat. But it works *some*, Sid. I did try it . . . Do you think the FTC would let them just put anything on the air . . . like that . . . ?

SIDNEY. (*soothingly—but with maddening assurance*) Baby—

IRIS. (*shrieking and breaking free—as the old comforting relation threatens again*) I DON'T WANT TO PLAY APPALACHIAN ANY MORE!

---

*See p. 132.

SIDNEY. All right, honey, but there's no reason to get all tied up in new games, Iris . . .

IRIS. (*shaking her head violently*) You don't understand, you still don't understand! I am not the same . . . I am different . . .

SIDNEY. (*laughing, with wonder*) Dear, sweet God . . . I've been living with a little girl . . . a child . . .

IRIS. Sidney, *one* of us here is a child and it's not me! . . . I've found out plenty about the world in the last few weeks, and it's nothing like you—or Papa—want it to be. . . . It's not! It's not! There are things talked about, laughed about while you stand there framed by that sign . . . that make me wonder how I ever thought you knew anything about this world at all! *This* world, Sidney! It's so dirty.

SIDNEY. (*rising and crossing to her again*) And what I am trying to tell you, little girl, is that you are learning the cynicism bit at the wrong time in our lives . . . (*He is gesturing toward the sign in the window. The crowd outside is heard again, muffled CHEERS and the CAMPAIGN SONG.*) We *won* something today, Iris. Not much . . . just a little part of the world turned right side up . . .

IRIS. (*the final outpouring*) *Sidney! Stop it! I can't stand it!* You haven't won anything—they're all the same people!

SIDNEY. What are you talking about?

IRIS. I'm talking about real life, Sidney. The people you've been fighting, they *own* Wally: the house he lives in, the clothes on his back, the toothpaste he uses! They *own* him, utterly, completely, entirely!

SIDNEY. (*frantically shaking his head* "no"—*but his eyes saying* "yes") What kind of psychotic filth is this!

IRIS. It *is* filth. You cannot *imagine* what filth. But it's not psychotic. Oh Jesus, I wish it were. But it's not. Sidney, haven't you noticed anything in the last weeks—they didn't spend fifteen cents to stop Wally! Didn't you *notice*! Jesus, I have met people who couldn't *believe* you're not in on it. Oh Sid. Sid, I tried to tell you, but *you*— (*helplessly*) Anyhow, in a few months he'll be having press conferences to explain how the pinkos and bohemians duped him in the first place and how he has found his way back to the "tried and true leadership of the . . . mother party!" (*She starts out, walking very much like the dead, picking up her bags. As she opens the door, the triumphant sounds of the RALLY fill the room.*) I would stay with you awhile now if it would help anything. But it wouldn't. (*turning, stone-faced*) I'll pick up my things some time this week. Tell Gloria I'll call her on a break. (*Then, suddenly:*) For God's sake, Sidney, take down that sign! It's like spit in your face! (*She exits* D.R. *The SIGN pulses with a life of its own; the roar of the CROWD grows louder. SIDNEY reaches up and clutches the sign for a long moment as the tension builds; he jerks it loose at one end—but then releases it. Very much like a blind man, he moves to the drawing board where his hand takes up the yardstick—the "sword of his ancestors"—which he draws and holds aloft before him, in duplication of the prior scene, saluting a foe that cannot be cut down . . . then lets it slip through his fingers.*)

DIMOUT

Scene 4

TIME: *Several hours later.*

AT RISE: *Except for the MOONLIGHT, the apartment is dark, the place a mess. SIDNEY lies stretched out under the coffee table, in considerable pain; one hand clutches at a center spot in his lower chest. An open whiskey bottle is near. In rough spasms, he harshly half milks/half mocks the plaintive notes of an old Yiddish melody,* "Rozhankes Mit Mandlen." *His sister-in-law GLORIA crosses on from* D.L. *carrying a small piece of luggage. She is about 26, as lovely as we have heard, but with surprising, fresh-faced, wholesome, "all-American" looks: with her bag she reminds one of a coed home for the week-end and no other thing. She knocks at the door; he stirs, says nothing. Finally she tries it and comes in.*

GLORIA. (*quizzically looking about in the shadows*) Sidney? Iris? (*sets down her bag and turns on a LAMP*)

SIDNEY. (*roaring drunk*) Stop it . . . Let there be darkness! . . . Let the tides of night envelop and protect us from the light! . . . How do you like them apples, Goethe, old baby? Let there be darkness, I say! Out, I say! (*then, recognizing her*) Gloria!

GLORIA. (*laughing*) You're a nut!

SIDNEY. Gloria! (*She picks him up—drags him to couch.*)

GLORIA. Where's Iris?

SIDNEY. (*blankly*) Iris? . . . Oh, *Iris* . . . my wife! (*Singing* "The Fireship"* *in reply: it is a song about a prostitute.*)

"She had a dark and roving eye!
And her hair hung down in ring-el-ets!

(*He folds over and rather gags with pain.*)

A nice girl, a proper girl—
But one of the roving kind!"

---

*See p. 136.

GLORIA. You're having an attack—aren't you? (*GLORIA thinks of it, then crosses to the refrigerator and gets container of milk, turning on LAMP over the counter as she goes.*)

SIDNEY. (*flat on back, top of lungs*)

"And her hair hung down in ring-el-lets!
A nice girl, a proper girl—"

GLORIA. (*offering the milk*) Come on, Sidney, drink this. (*SIDNEY drinks, expecting liquor—spits out the whole mouthful and makes a face.*) What's going on, Sidney?

SIDNEY. Can it be that the fall of man has entirely escaped even *your* notice?

GLORIA. What are you talking about?

SIDNEY. All that sweat! All that up-all-night! All that, you should pardon the allusion—(*hissing out the word*) *Passion!* All for a mere flunky of Power. (*gaily*) Who cares anyhow? The world likes itself just fine the way it is, so don't pick at it. That's all you gotta know about anything: Don't pick at it! (*He opens the door and bellows up.*) Hey, Orpheus, come on down: I'm ready to cross over the Styx. (*He mugs heavily at GLORIA.*) Get it: I'm just going to hell with myself!

GLORIA. You need looking after. Where *is* Iris?

SIDNEY. Who? Oh, her again. Who the hell knows. Iris was one of the lesser goddesses anyway. A kind of "girl Friday" for Zeus, who has run off to capture lightning bolts on account of it pays well and you get to meet all the up-and-coming young gods and things. (*sudden thought*) Hey, lookit me! Who am I? (*Posing on couch in god-like stance; GLORIA can only laugh.*) Come on, who am I? (*confidentially*) I'll give you a hint: I am *not* Apollo. In fact, I am not a god. (*Jimmy Durante imitation, self-mocking*) *I*gnore my stately bearing and look in my eyes— (*circus barker, arm aloft*) and you will see there unmistakable mortality! Who am I? (*collapses*) I'm Modern Man: flat on my back with— (*grandly taking stock of his assets*) an oozing intestine, a bit of a tear— (*dabs eye with one finger and holds it up*) frozen in the corner of my eye . . . (*false enthusiasm, sitting up*) a glass of booze which will saturate without alleviating . . . (*peers blindly out in benign confusion*) and not the dimmest notion of what it is all about . . . (*flourish and bow; sings loudly.*)

"Oh, we're lost out here in the stars—!"

(*During this DAVID has come downstairs.*)

DAVID. (*entering coolly*) Well, I see I have entered in a large moment.

SIDNEY. David, my boy! The only man I know personally who is unafraid of the dark! (*tosses him bottle without warning*) Have a drink.

DAVID. (*catching it*) You're drunk and silly and I have a guest. (*starts out*)

SIDNEY. Well, bring her—excuse me—*him* down and we'll have a happening or something.

DAVID. We're already having one, thank you.

SIDNEY. You knew it all along, didn't you, Cassandra? (*grabbing hold of him*) All that motion, all that urgency . . . all for nothing?! That's the whole show, isn't it? A great plain where neither the wind blows, nor the rain falls, nor anything else happens. *Really happens*, I mean. Besides our arriving and one day leaving . . . That's what your plays are about, aren't they?

DAVID. Well, at least you are learning.

SIDNEY. Oh yes! And to laugh! To laugh! Because you're right about everything! (*sings*)

"Little stars . . . big stars . . .
Oh, we're lost out here in—"

(*turning as if seeing her for the first time*) Gloria! (*He holds out his arms. She goes to him and they embrace; there is a quite genuine affection between these two. He holds her rather desperately and, inadvertently, hurts her.*) What's the matter?

GLORIA. (*covers quickly*) Some bruises. It's all right. Are *you* all right? (*SIDNEY beams, hiccups, then grabs his mouth; starts for the bathroom with great dignity which he cannot sustain—he breaks and runs in, closing door behind him. She digs a cigarette out of her bag and notes DAVID fully for the first time.*) And you must be—

DAVID. David Ragin. Hi.

GLORIA. (*with recognition; coming towards him warmly*) From upstairs. Hi. I'm—

DAVID. Gloria. The sister who—"travels a lot." (*as she clearly reacts and halts*) Oh, it's all right. I practically live here and it's, like, all in the family, no secrets. I do naughty things with boys only—so relax. (*lights a match for her*)

GLORIA. (*pointedly using her own lighter*) You're very free with personal information.

DAVID. Isn't it the great tradition for writers and whores to share the world's truths?

GLORIA. (*spinning with astonishment*) Listen, I don't like your language—or you.

DAVID. I'm sorry. I didn't know it would upset you.

GLORIA. Weren't you leaving? (*She turns away.*)

DAVID. I said I was sorry. And I almost never apologize to anyone. I apologized to you—because I respect you.

GLORIA. I said, weren't you leaving?

DAVID. Look—it's okay with me. Relax. I'm writing about a—girl like you. I cut away all the hypocrisy—

GLORIA. (*vehemently*) Look little boy—I've never met you before, but I know everything you are about to say, because it's been asked and written four thousand times . . . Anything I tell you, you'd believe it and put it down and feel like you'd been close to something old and deep and wise. Any bunch of lies I make up. Well, these are not office hours. Now get the hell out of here! (*Rising, she winces and catches her side.*)

DAVID. Are you hurt?

GLORIA. (*in pain as she crosses to bar*) Please be some kind of gentleman if you think you can *swing* it— (*a gibe at his homosexuality*) and go away.

DAVID. Can I get you something?

GLORIA. Just go away!

(*He exits upstairs. SIDNEY re-enters, his head and shirt doused with water, affecting sobriety to little avail. Slowly, stiffly, with the dignity of the soused, he crosses to GLORIA at the bar, carrying one shoe.*)

SIDNEY. (*at the bottle*) Want a drink? Oh, I always forget—about you and your face, the tissues and all.

GLORIA. (*slapping playfully at the underchin and cheeks*) It's all right. Let the damn tissues fall! (*takes the glass; looking up at him, softly*) I've quit, Sid. *Really* quit.

SIDNEY. (*changing the subject*) How did you—hurt yourself?

GLORIA. Oh, that's the result of an evening with six and one half feet of psycho. My analyst insists I have a predi—what do you call it?

SIDNEY. Predilection?

GLORIA. Predilection for psychos and vice cops. This last one . . . I think he was trying to kill me. (*rises; looking around*) This place is a wreck! When's Iris coming?

SIDNEY. She'll be along.

GLORIA. (*grinning*) Hey—Sid, lookit me! (*holding up the glass triumphantly*) Whiskey. I've joined the human race. No more goofball pills—I'm kicking everything. (*She makes a comic face and their glasses clink.*) I did the whole gooey farewell bit with some of the kids. Adios, Muchachas! I'm going to marry him. Yes, I mean *after* we talk about it. I wouldn't unless I told him. I know girls who've done that. Doesn't work out: you run into people. Never works out. I'm going to sit down and tell him— (*A swinging, breezy recitation brimming over with confidence to conceal the lack of it: rehearsed too many times to perfection because she knows it won't work.*) "I was a nineteen-year-old package of fluff from Trenersville, Nowhere, and I met this nothing who took one look at this baby face of mine and said, 'Honey, there's a whole special market for you. Slink is on the way out; all-American wholesomeness is the rage. You'll be part of the aristocracy of the profession!'" Which is true. Only they don't exactly describe the profession. After that you develop your own rationales: (a) "It's old as time anyhow!" (*They clink glasses loudly and laugh.*) (b)— (*hand on heart—for God and country*) "It's a service to society!" (*They clink again.*) and (c) "The *real* prostitutes are everybody else; especially housewives and career girls." (*Again they howl.*) We trade those gems back and forth for hours. Nobody believes it, but it helps on the bad days. And, sweetie, there are a lot of bad days.

SIDNEY. Gloria—no matter what happens, honey, you've got to stick to that.

GLORIA. (*Glass poised in midair, she lowers it slowly.*) Okay, Sid, what is it—a letter or a phonograph record with violins?

SIDNEY. Gloria—

GLORIA. (*stands; sets drink on coffee table; a supreme effort at self-control: to both steel herself for—and hold off—the inevitable*) I was on this date once, Sid. He had a book of reproductions by Goya. And there was this one—an etching, I think. Have you ever seen it? There's this woman, a Spanish peasant woman, and she's standing like this—reaching out. And what she's reaching for are the teeth of a dead man. A man who'd been hanged. And she is rigid with—revulsion, but she wants his teeth, because it said in the book that in those days people thought that the teeth of the dead were good luck. Can you imagine that? The things some people think they have to do? To *survive* in this world? (*a beat; lightly*) Some day I'm going to buy that print. It's all about my life . . .

SIDNEY. He loves you, honey. He loves you terribly . . .

GLORIA. (*Demanding the letter with tough, hoarse, urgency: she is ready for it now.*) Come on, Sidney!

(*SIDNEY hands her letter and she turns away to read it. There is presently in the silence only the single hurt outcry of any small creature of the forest, mortally struck. She crumples it.*)

SIDNEY. (*pouring a drink fast and trying to push it on her*) Come on—drink this for me—

GLORIA. Get that out of my face, Sidney! (*She knocks it away and rises; he tries to block this.*) Get out of my way, Sidney. (*pulling free with a mighty jerk*) Let go! (*She gets her bag and downs pills.*) You see, no fuss, no muss . . . Drugs are the coming thing, Sid. (*The reversion is progressive: she is pushing hard for it, not waiting on the pills, and drinking also.*) Ha—you want to hear something! I was going to *marry* that vanilla dinge! Do you know what some of the girls do? They go off and they sleep with a colored boy—and I mean *any* colored boy so long as he is black—because that is the one bastard who can't look down on them five seconds after it's over! And I was going to *marry* one!

SIDNEY. (*crossing to GLORIA*) Maybe he'll change his mind. He was sort of in a state of shock. I mean, try to understand about Alton—

GLORIA. Oh, so he's in a state of shock! Oh Jesus, that yellow-faced bastard! *He*'s shocked! Look, Sid, I'll bet you two to one that at this instant he is lying dead drunk in the arms of the blondest or blackest two-bit hooker in town. *Nursing* his shock! Telling his tale of woe! *His* tale! And she'll be telling it somewhere by morning to the girls and roaring with laughter. Like I'm doing! . . . Aw, what the hell am I carrying on for—the life beats the hell out of that nine-to-five jazz— (*Suddenly, without pause or warning, a violent sob.*) *SIDNEY! WHAT HAPPENED TO MY LIFE!?* (*He tries to go to her; she holds up a hand to stay him.*) I'll be twenty-six this winter and I have tried to kill myself three times since I was twenty-three . . . I was always awkward . . . But I'll make it. (*Leans head back to compose herself for a long moment; then:*) Well . . . that's enough gloom and doom, everybody! Come on, Sidney brother, cheer up! (*She ruffles his hair, nuzzles playfully in a desperate effort at gaiety and release. Weaving toward the phonograph:*) Let's have some music. And none of that creepy stuff my creepy father used to play. (*She puts on a RECORD —some very modern jazz, cool and eerie, throbbing and intense; starts to dance.*) Yeah . . . that's good. I have to have music . . . It closes things out . . . Come on, Sidney brother— (*She flicks off LAMP, beckons and, as MOONLIGHT fills the room, SIDNEY moves into her arms. They dance in a tight embrace, he in a bemused and delicious half-stupor; she as if, in the mere physical body contact, she were clinging to life. Now the mood of the scene begins to heighten as per their state—a disintegration of reality to match their world's. A LIGHT, deathly blue, of great transparency, settles slowly, then gives way to a hot and sensual FUCHSIA. The MUSIC follows suit—the more familiar jazz sounds going even beyond their own definitions. When each speaks, it is stiffly and unnaturally—"happy" drunk—with a quality of disconnected revelation, an inspired fragmented delivery, as if lucidity no longer required logic.*) Things as they are . . . are as they are . . . and have been and will be that way . . . because they got that way . . . because things were as they were in the first place!

(*Above them, DAVID has entered and slowly descended the stairs, glancing behind him several times. Halfway down, he stands—in silhouette—smoking thoughtfully.*)

SIDNEY. "Society is based on complicity in the common crime! We all suffer from the murder of the primal father who kept all the females for himself—and drove the sons away . . . (*DAVID continues down and watches at window or open door as the heat, half sensual, half poetic, mounts between them.*) "So we murdered him and—cannibals that we are— (*spaced out with the blissful "discovery"*) WE ATE HIM!" (*He "devours" her neck. They kiss tentatively, then hungrily.*)

DAVID. (*leaning against doorjamb; delighted*) Sidney, you've finally joined the human race! Welcome to the club!

SIDNEY. (*to DAVID*) We are *all* guilty!

DAVID. (*nodding*) Therefore all guilt is *equal*!

GLORIA. (*beckoning to him*) Therefore, *none* are innocent.

DAVID. (*crossing to join them*) Therefore—

ALL. *No one* is guilty!

SIDNEY. (*does a soft-shoe turn and freeze*) Any two of anyone . . .

GLORIA. (*follows suit*) . . . advocating anything . . .

DAVID. (*follows suit*) . . . is imposing on the rest of us!

ALL. *Totalitarianism!* (*The beat throbs and the three dance the Frug, Watusi, Twist, etc.*)

GLORIA. It is right and natural for the individual to be primarily concerned with himself!

DAVID. He must be dedicated to his own interests.

SIDNEY. (*inspired*) There is a *revolution* in this idea! (*SIDNEY lies down on couch as DAVID melts into GLORIA's beckoning arms. They dance.*)

GLORIA. Whaddaya do if your own father calls you a tramp . . . on his deathbed . . . huh? Whaddaya do?

SIDNEY. (*on his back, rousing, with a flourish*) You only *think* that flowers smell good. 'Tis an illusion!

DAVID. Trying to live with your father's values can kill you. Ask me, I know.

GLORIA. No, Sweetie, living *without* your father's values can kill you. Ask *me*, *I* know.

SIDNEY. (*sits up, cross-legged, Zen Buddhist fashion; stereotypic "oriental" sing-song; pantomines:*) Take a needle thus. (*from lapel; large gesture*) Peer through the eye. As much as you can see will be a part of the world. But it will be a *true* part, will it not? Therefore, set down what you have seen and call it—*The* Truth! If anyone argues with you, explain to the fool that it is harder to look *through* a needle than to look *around* one. (*He flops back.*)

DAVID. Any pretension of concern for decency is the most indecent of all human affectations.

GLORIA. And besides, how many things can a nice, normal, healthy American girl kick at one time—the racket and the pills? And take on integration too?

SIDNEY. (*sits bolt upright; declaiming:*) To be or not to be! (*A great pause; he sears us with his eyes—and falls back.*) Well, better leave *that* one alone!

(*As SIDNEY dozes off on the sofa, GLORIA stops DAVID with a long wet kiss, then steps back as the MUSIC comes to an abrupt halt and the surreal FUCHSIA fades back to MOONLIGHT.*)

GLORIA. Where's the music . . . ? What happened to the music?

DAVID. Don't let's stop! . . . It was mah-velous! We were so completely outside ourselves.

GLORIA. (*crossing to phonograph*) Sure, baby, a drunk, a hophead, and a sick little boy could conjure up the Last Supper if they wanted. (*She turns it on and crosses to bar for a refill. The MUSIC throbs softly.*)

DAVID. (*following her*) No, listen. (*Leads her to a seat and kneels before her or draws her head back against him; with wistful melancholy and some difficulty: he is embarrassed, but must get through to her. We should see his face.*) All your life you want certain things and when you try to trace them back with the finger of your mind to where you first started to want them, there is nothing but a haze . . . I was seven. So was Nelson. We used to play all day in my yard. He had fine golden hair and a thin delicate profile— (*He traces her features in outline with the fingers of one hand, touches her hair.*) and Mother always said: "Nelson is a real aristocrat." Then, just like that, one summer his family moved to Florence, Italy. And I never saw him again.

GLORIA. (*reaching out compassionately to touch his cheek*) And you've been looking for him ever since.

DAVID. Yes.

GLORIA. And now?

DAVID. There is a beautiful burnished golden boy very much like Nelson sitting on a chair upstairs. He is from one of the oldest, finest families in New England. He is exquisite. But great damage has been done to him—

GLORIA. (*Stiffening; for this girl there are no surprises left.*) He requires . . . the presence of a woman. (*She crosses away* DS.)

DAVID. Not just any woman—

GLORIA. (*Nodding; she has heard it all before; not looking at him.*) Someone young enough, fresh enough, in certain light, to make him think it is somebody of his own class . . .

DAVID. Yes. But—you don't have to do anything. Apparently—it is merely a matter of—watching.

GLORIA. (*raising her eyes pathetically as SIDNEY rolls over on the couch*) And *you're* a friend of Sidney's . . .

DAVID. (*coming closer*) It's not for me. If he asked for the snows of the Himalayas tonight, I would try to get it for him. I thought you might—know of such things.

GLORIA. Oh . . . I—know of such things!

DAVID. Will you come up—?

GLORIA. (*A long beat as she fights for composure. Then, still not looking at him:*) Sure . . . why not?

DAVID. It's apartment 3-F.

(*He goes out and up. She stands for a moment, then crosses quickly to phonograph, which she turns up louder, as if to drown out some voice within her. She tries to dance a little; that doesn't work. She downs more pills with liquor. Touches up make-up. Then, snapping her fingers and undulating to the MUSIC—with a fixed smile—she goes out. But as she mounts the third step, she freezes in the grip of a physical revulsion—and suddenly whirls back, shouting: her words a single guttural cry of pain.*)

GLORIA. SICK PEOPLE BELONG IN HOSPITALS!!! (*For a moment her eyes dart frantically and she whimpers, trapped, seeking refuge. There is none. She crosses to SIDNEY, shakes him.*) Sidney . . . (*He does not respond. She shakes him again.*) Sidney, brother, wake up . . . (*cajoling*) C'mon, Sidney . . . (*He sleeps on. As she crosses for a drink, her eyes find the bottle of pills—she considers a moment, rejects the idea, retreats into the beat of the music. But the bottle is a magnet. At last she makes up her mind and empties it into her hand, her purse falling onto the floor. Resolutely, almost calmly:*) Papa—I *am* better than this! (*She crosses to the bathroom clutching the pills; halts, terrified at the unseen presence there; but then, with a final lift of her head, enters and closes the door. PHONE begins to ring. On the 4th ring the LIGHTS slowly dim. SIDNEY sleeps on as the PHONE rings on and on . . .*)

DIMOUT

SCENE 5

TIME: *Early the next morning.*
AT RISE: *There is now a stark, businesslike and cold atmosphere in the apartment. It is early dawn; in the course of this scene the blue-gray of the hour slowly lifts, until, at the end, the sun breaks full. IRIS sits in the rocker slumped in her coat, hands in pockets, eyes red and staring off at nothing in particular. The bathroom door stands ajar. SIDNEY enters from the street.*

SIDNEY. I got them a cab! Fred'll call the doctor and have Mavis sedated. (*IRIS says nothing.*) Let it come, honey. Let it out. Cry. It's worse if you do what you're doing . . . (*He spots GLORIA's purse where she had dropped it, picks it up and stands looking at the bathroom, then turns away—with face contorted—to face his wife. A long beat; then, helplessly:*) Want a cup of tea or something? (*WALLY appears at the open door, knocks. A beat; SIDNEY just looks at him. He comes in.*)

WALLY. Sid, I came as soon as I—

SIDNEY. (*evenly*) The primary is over, O'Hara. We *lost.* (*He turns away. WALLY ignores it, crosses to IRIS, putting hat on table.*)

WALLY. I heard about—your sister. If there's anything I can do. . . . (*IRIS does not respond in any way.*) She's in bad shape, Sidney. Why don't you call a doctor? (*Without looking at him, SIDNEY just hands him his hat.*) I know, Sidney. You think I'm the prince of all the bastards.

SIDNEY. No, as a matter of fact you exaggerate: I'd say you're a rather rank-and-file bastard. Good morning, O'Hara.

WALLY. Sidney, it's not like you think it is—

SIDNEY. Nothing ever is. (*indicating the door*)

WALLY. Look, Sid, this is *me. Wally.* Do you think I would have gone along with them if there was another way? I haven't changed on you, Sid. I'm the same man. Only I've had to face up to something finally: in order to get anything done, anything at all in this world, baby—

SIDNEY. —"You've got to know where the power is."

WALLY. (*shrugs*) That's the way it's always been, that's the way it always will be.

SIDNEY. I see. And besides— (*softly; fingering GLORIA's purse and recalling her words*) "All the real prostitutes are everybody else."

WALLY. Name calling is the last refuge of ineffectuals. You rage and I function. Think about that sometime, Sid. (*crossing to the window*) Look, you know that stop sign that the housewives have been trying to get at Hudson and Leroy Streets? With the baby carriage demonstrations and the petitions and all? Well, they'll get their stop sign now. *I'll* get it for them. But not as some wide-eyed reformer. And better garbage collection and the new playground and a lot of other things too.

SIDNEY. And Willie Johnson, O'Hara? How's about the narcotics traffic . . . and the police?

WALLY. That's more complicated. You don't go jumping into things.

SIDNEY. I see: we can go on stepping over the bodies of the junkies, but the trains will run on time! (*He clicks his heels and throws off the Fascist salute.*)

WALLY. Well, as a matter of fact I knew it would be like this. That you would be standing there with that exact expression on your face: filled with all the simple self-righteousness of bleeding innocence again debauched! (*He's done with restraint.*) It must feel good, eh, Sid? To be able to judge! One good betrayal vindicates all our own crimes, doesn't it? Well, I'm going to tell you something I learned a long time ago. "If you want to survive—"

SIDNEY. (*swiftly as if by rote*) "—you've got to swing the way the world swings!"

WALLY. (*angry*) Exactly. You either *negotiate* or get out of the race!

SIDNEY. (*looking at him curiously; a beat; then, eyes lighting:*) I see. Your friends don't waste time, do they? Thanks, pal. Message delivered.

WALLY. Sidney, what are you talking about?

SIDNEY. (*without warning: the real confrontation*) They're after my paper now, aren't they, O'Hara?

WALLY. (*Thrown: he would have preferred this on his own ground. Indicating Iris:*) Sidney, this is not a good time.

SIDNEY. It's the perfect time.

WALLY. You don't understand. They don't want anything. Nothing changes. I've made them understand that. You go on as you've always wanted . . .

SIDNEY. You mean covering the art shows? Doing charming little photographic essays of the snow on our quaint streets? Yes? (*WALLY nods.*) And leave the *world*—to you?

WALLY. It's not like that. The world needs people like you—to do what you do best. To raise our sights. You have a gift, man, an instinct—for writing—for music—ideas. You turn people on.

SIDNEY. Right. But what if at some point I choose to write about *other* things . . . say, for example—"*them*"?

WALLY. Sidney, "they" didn't do you in. You did yourself in and there ought to be a lesson in it for you: stay up in the mountains with your banjos and your books where you belong.

SIDNEY. Yes, but suppose I don't want to. Suppose I'm obtuse. Suppose I *refuse*?

WALLY. Sidney, make sense. What *for*? The election's a formality now. You know that.

SIDNEY. Sure. (*repeating*) But suppose I refuse?

WALLY. Sidney, I'm talking to you as a friend . . .

SIDNEY. *Suppose I refuse?*

WALLY. (*reluctantly*) Then the paper won't last six months.

SIDNEY. (*stares at him; bitter laughter; then:*) Six months. A lot can happen in six months . . .

WALLY. I mean it, Sidney.

SIDNEY. Oh, *I* mean it, too! Man, don't you know what kind of house you just walked into? Didn't Death breathe on you as you came through the door? I don't think you understand what really happened here last night— (*For the first time IRIS stirs.*) I'm sorry, honey, but I have to . . . You see, Wally, Gloria didn't *die*— (*WALLY looks at him oddly.*) Old people die . . . seasons die . . . flowers die. But Gloria—you never did get to meet Gloria, did you? Well, Gloria was a girl who "swung the way the world swings." A girl who bought the whole package—everything you stand for—

WALLY. Now just a damn minute—

SIDNEY. Everything you stand for! And last night while I lay stoned on that couch, that girl— (*His voice breaks and he cannot go on. A beat as he struggles.*) While I lay there in a drunken stupor— (*He is unable to continue.*)

WALLY. Sidney, I really have to go. What is it that you're trying to say?

SIDNEY. That I'm going to fight you, O'Hara.

WALLY. Sidney, you're overwrought. We'll talk about it tomorrow. (*turns to go*)

SIDNEY. We'll talk about it *now.* I'm going to fight you, O'Hara, because I have to. Because I know something now and I have to live with it: the fact that my sister is dead because for a little while last night *I bought the package too.* Don't you understand, man? The slogans of capitulation can KILL! Every time we say "Live and let live"—death triumphs! Too much has happened, too much has happened to me. I love my wife—I want her back. I loved my sister—I'd like to see her alive. I love Alton. I loved Willie Johnson. I—I love *you.* I wish—I wish it could all be different . . . but no way! That which warped and distorted all of us is— (*suddenly lifting his hands as if this were literally true*) all around: it is in this very air! This swirling, seething madness that you ask us to help maintain! It's no good, Wally—your world. It's no—damn—good! You have forced me to take a position. Finally—the one thing I never wanted to do. (*shrugs*) Just not being *for* you is not enough. To live, to breathe—I've got to be against you.

WALLY. (*the genuine passion of the compromised*) My friend, you *reek* of innocence!

IRIS. (*suddenly, turning*) The question is, Wally, what is it *you* reek of?

SIDNEY. I'll tell you what he reeks of. He reeks of—no, read it in the next issue, Iris. Six months? Isn't that what you said, Wally? Six months? Thirty-two issues—

IRIS. (*in spite of herself*) Twenty-six, Sidney . . .

SIDNEY. (*He looks at her:* "you sure?" *She nods. He shrugs.*) Twenty-six issues. Goodbye, O'Hara. I'll see you again. Only let me warn you: this time, thanks to you, I'll be tougher—more seasoned—harder to deceive—

WALLY. (*with genuine wonder*) Sidney, you really are a fool . . .

SIDNEY. (*nodding*) Always have been. A fool who believes that— (*His eyes find his wife's as he fights to restrain the tears.*) death is waste and love is sweet and that the earth turns and men change every day and that rivers run and that people want to be better than they are and that flowers smell good and that I hurt terribly today, and that hurt is desperation and desperation is— energy and energy can *move* things . . .

WALLY. (*looking from one to the other*) Let me know the time and place of the funeral. I'd like to send flowers. (*WALLY starts out, adjusts his hat, notes the Sign, gazes at them, and exits* D.R. *There is a long moment of silence. IRIS rises. She does not look at SIDNEY.*)

IRIS. For a long time I've been wanting something. I think it was for us to be all of ourselves. You and me. To find and know and be all of ourselves. (*turning to him at last*) I want to come home, Sidney. I want to come home, but . . .

SIDNEY. We'll talk about it. (*She crosses to the bathroom and with a supreme mustering of will, and her whole body, pushes the door shut, as if on the Past, and leans with her back against it. SIDNEY looks at her, helpless to staunch the pain.*) Iris—

IRIS. Sidney, don't tear yourself apart. I know you loved her . . . (*She crosses to him; holding her hands before her and turning them slowly.*) When she was little . . . she had fat, pudgy hands . . . and I used to have to scrub them . . . because she couldn't get them clean. And so I would pretend that they were fish and I was the Fish Lady cleaning those little fish to sell them. That always tickled her so, and she would laugh and laugh and— (*She gags on the first great sob, he folds her into his arms and the tears come freely now.*)

SIDNEY. Yes . . . weep, darling. Weep. Let us both weep. That is the first thing: to let ourselves feel again . . . and then, tomorrow, we shall make something strong of this sorrow . . . (*They sit spent and motionless as the clear light of MORNING fills the room.*)

CURTAIN

VILLAGE INTELLECT REVEALED*

By Lorraine Hansberry

Some years back a friend of mine called to say she was subjected to mental harassment because she had in her window a certain political poster that exhorted its readers in behalf of the opposition of the then entrenched and powerful regular machine in her district.

Her reaction to this captivated me immediately. She was an utterly apolitical transplanted Westerner with a twanging and seemingly indifferent accent on life whom I took to be the unlikeliest person in the world to be found locked in some point-making struggle with big-city politics. And I was captivated because I had been brought up on World War II movies, and her reaction was exactly what it would have been in a wartime movie: she wasn't about to be threatened into removing that sign. Her Mr.-Smith-Goes-to-Washington pioneer marrow had risen to the occasion. Naturally, I sat down to write a rather obvious play about the incident: Oklahoma stubbornness, in conflict with oily New York political conformity, triumphs.

Inevitably, if you know playwrights, the play and my interest in it shifted over the years as I worked at it. It stopped being preoccupied with my friend's quaint character to a point where she dropped out of the play altogether to be replaced by another character who, more

---

*Reprinted from *The New York Times*, October 11, 1964.

and more, as the play became obsessed with the problem of political commitment in general, came to dominate the work. That character's name was, through a process of evolution, Sidney Brustein.

Few things are more natural than that the tortures of the engagé should attract me thematically. Being 34 years old at this writing means that I am of the generation that grew up in the swirl and dash of the Sartre-Camus debate of the post-war years. The silhouette of the Western intellectual poised in hesitation before the flames of involvement was an accurate symbolism of some of my closest friends, some of whom crossed each other leaping in and out, for instance, of the Communist party. Others searched, as agonizingly, for some ultimate justification of their lives in the abstractions flowing out of London or Paris. Still others were contorted into seeking a meaningful repudiation of *all* justifications of anything and had, accordingly, turned to Zen, action painting or even just Jack Kerouac.

Play's Core

Mine is, after all, the generation that came to maturity drinking in the forebodings of the Silones, Koestlers and Richard Wrights. It had left us ill-prepared for decisions that had to be made in our own time about Algeria, Birmingham or the Bay of Pigs. By the 1960's, few enough American intellectuals had it within them to be ashamed that their discovery of the "betrayal" of the Cuban Revolution by Castro just happened to coincide with the change of heart of official American Government policy. They left it to TV humorists to defend the Agrarian Reform in the end. It is the climate and mood of such intellectuals, if not those particular events, which constitute the core of a play called "The Sign in Sidney Brustein's Window."

It is a play about a nervous, ulcerated, banjo-making young man in whom I see an embodiment of a certain kind of Greenwich Village intellectual as I have known him during the ten years of my life that I lived in that community.

Stage Intellectuals

In fact, it was my hope in the writing of this particular play to "do something" about stage intellectuals (as, indeed, I once hoped that I might "do something" about stage Negroes). The American theater (and motion pictures) concept of an "intellectual," it seems to me, is someone who wears horn-rimmed glasses and exceedingly attractive tweed sports jackets and speaks in stilted phrases until they are shown true "life" by some earthy mess of a girl in black stockings.

The corduroy-wearing chukka-booted, Bergman film-loving, non-cold water flat living, New School lecture-attending, Washington Square concert-going, middle class and usually Jewish, argument-loving Greenwich Village intellectual has rarely peopled our stage in his full dimension. It is my belief that "The Sign in Sidney Brustein's Window" fills in something of a genuine portrait of the milieu. . . .

RUNNING PROP LIST

KITCHEN:

In Refrigerator:

Container of milk
Plastic bag
  Lettuce (washed)
  One tomato
Two cans beer (Ballantine flip top)

On Refrigerator:

Electric coffee pot (to be filled)

On Shelf:

Can of coffee (open with dipper)
Salt and pepper (nice looking for table)
Flower vase (pencil in vase)
Small dish (spare letter underneath)
Stack of paper napkins

On Bar Counter:

Basket of apples (bread basket)
  Backstage underneath the basket
Four dishes stacked
Four forks wrapped in napkins
Four glasses (stacked two by two)
Ice bucket with ice
Bottle Scotch
Bottle Bourbon
Five highball glasses
Pack of cigarettes
Book of matches
Ash tray
Pack (5¢) Kleenex
Salad bowl (wooden with fork and spoon)

On Shelf under Counter:
Candlesticks with candles
Plastic silverware tray
Serving spoon in tray (for Paella)
Small cutting board
Sharp kitchen knife (on top)
Four highball glasses
Small kitchen foot pedal garbage can

WALL DOWN LEFT OF WINDOW:
Extra yardstick
Wallphone
Banjo
Election district map (2–2)

ON WINDOW SEAT:
Record player
Record on (Arm on record)
Pack of cigarettes
Book of matches
Ash tray
Pack of Kleenex
Book (South Pacific) (1–2)
On shelf below window seat
Empty record jacket

BEDROOM (off U.C.):
On shelf:
Stack of typing paper (1–2)
Chic shopping bag (2–3)
Shoe box with new shoes, Golden Girl Curl Box, and newspaper filler (ballast) at bottom
Large vinyl hat box (2–3)

BATHROOM (off U.R.):

U.S. *Shelf:*
Brown pill bottle (M&M's)

D.S. *Shelf:*
Glass of water
Glass with toothbrush
Open tube of toothpaste
Small pan of water (½ full)
Extra brown pill bottle (M&M's)

On Door:
Mirror
2 bath towels on rack

ON CONSOLE TABLE OR CHEST, NEAR DOOR:
Pack of cigarettes
Book of matches
Ash tray
Pack of Kleenex

ON ROCKER (Rocking Chair):
Volume of Thoreau
Three slips of paper to mark passages

ON DRAFTING TABLE:
Large pad tracing paper
Yardstick
Ash tray
Cigarbox containing:
Marking crayon
Cigarettes
Matches
Several pencils
Scotch tape

ON RACKS OF GLASSES (2–2):
Box of envelopes
Stack of mailing pieces

ON COUCH:
Two throw pillows

ON FLOOR BEHIND COUCH:
Iris's sneakers

ON COFFEE TABLE:
Large ash tray
Pack of cigarettes
Book of matches
Pack of Kleenex
Pencil
Five assorted magazines

OFF RIGHT PROP TABLE (by character):

SIDNEY:
Banner for window (set down near R. entrance for 1–2)

ALTON:
Bouquet of flowers (1–2)
Bottle of wine in newspaper bag (1–2)
Paperback book to throw at Iris (1–2)
Envelope with letter for Gloria (2–3)

IRIS:
Large grocery bag (1–1)
Two large cans tomato juice at bottom
Newspaper filler
Box of cookies
Box of soda crackers
Bottle of vinegar

Bottle of oil
Package wrapped to look like steak
New York Times
French bread
Pan of saffron rice (Paella) (1–2)
In large grocery bag (must be edible)
Airmail letter from Gloria (1–2)
(practical to be read)

WALLY:
3 or 4 Wally O'Hara posters
Cardboard of thumbtacks

MAX:
Art portfolio containing:
Masthead layout for newspaper
Large free form painting
Cigars

MAVIS:
Dress box (1–2) containing:
Black cocktail dress
Pocketbook containing:
Cigarette lighter
Cigarette case
Lipstick
Check for Sidney (2–3)

DAVID:
6 newspapers (2–2)
Sunglasses (2–2)
Matches (2–4)

OFF LEFT PROP TABLE (by character):

SIDNEY:
Set of keys

Two restaurant glass racks
Filled with glasses
Typed pages (Alton's newspaper story)
Rolled up American flag
(set down near L. entrance for 2–2)

ALTON:
Two restaurant glass racks
Filled with glasses
Glasses at center of top rack, clean for drinking
Two liquor bottles in top rack
Upstage corner slot of glass rack (empty)
Photo of Gloria
Picket signs (2–2)

WALLY:
Batch of political leaflets (2–2)
Picket signs (2–2)

MAX:
Picket signs (2–2)

GLORIA:
Luggage piece (2–4)
Purse containing
Bottle of pills
Cigarette case
Lighter

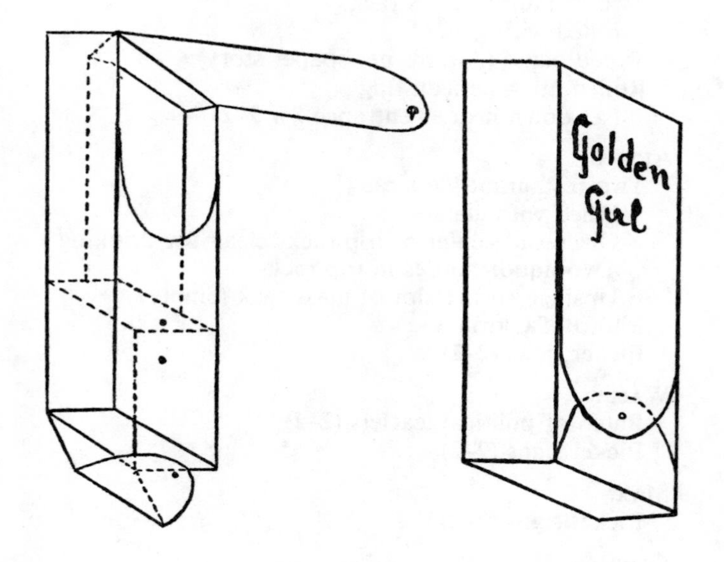

"Golden Girl" Curl Box (Act II, Scene 3)

The size of a large shoebox, it is constructed so that when Iris opens the top of the box (fastened with a single tack), the curlers tumble out of the trick bottom which is kept closed by the same tack. Plastic squeeze lotion bottle is cemented to shallow section.

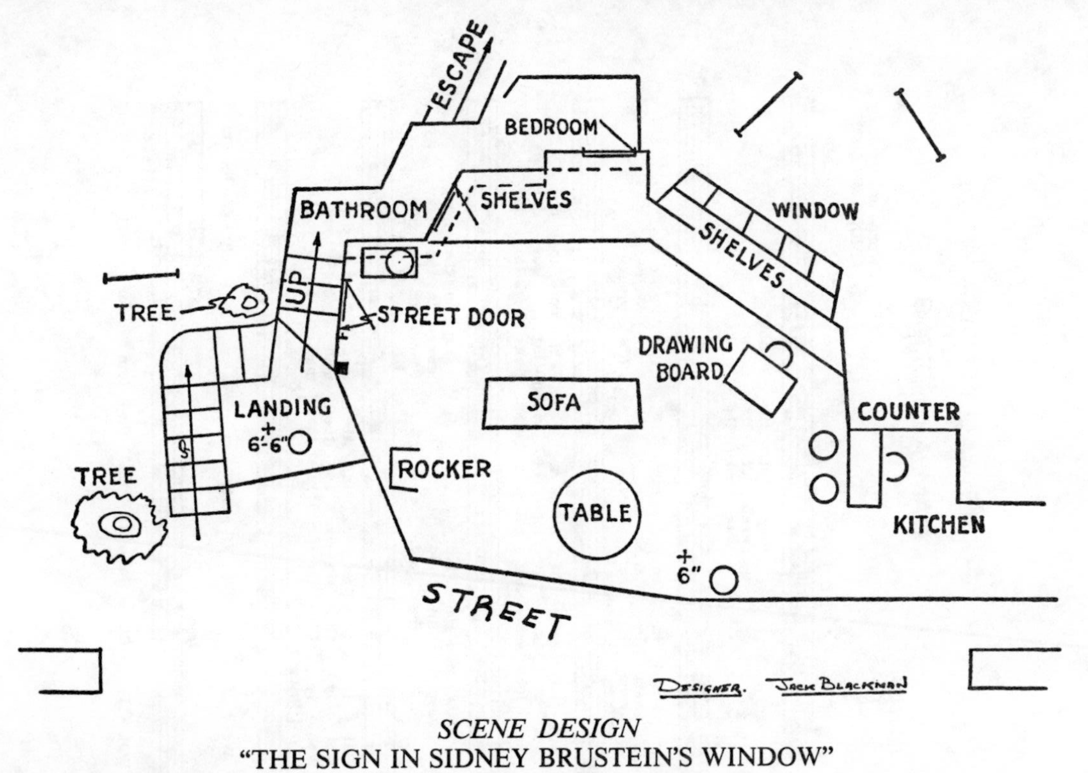

SCENE DESIGN
"THE SIGN IN SIDNEY BRUSTEIN'S WINDOW"

THE WALLY O'HARA CAMPAIGN SONG

Words and Music by
ERNIE SHELDON

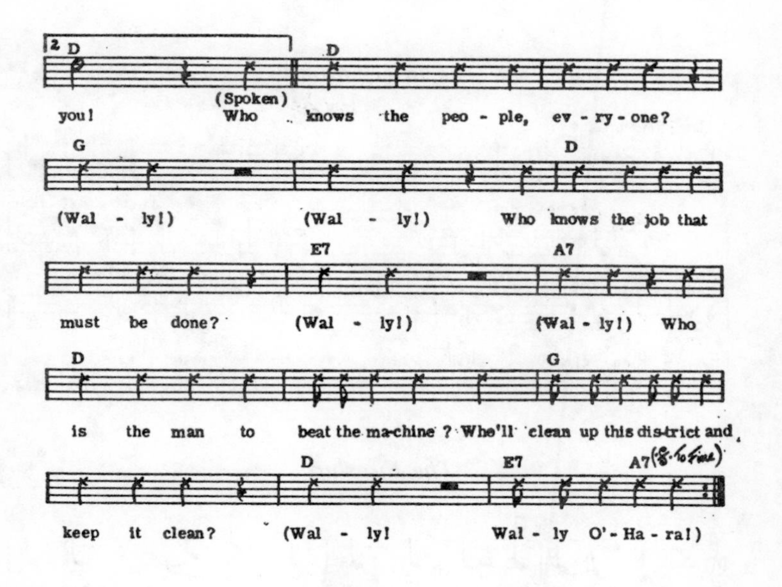
2
D
D
(Spoken)
you! Who knows the peo - ple, ev - ry - one?
G
D
(Wal - ly!) (Wal - ly!) Who knows the job that
E7
A7
must be done? (Wal - ly!) (Wal - ly!) Who
D
G
is the man to beat the ma-chine? Who'll clean up this dis-trict and
D
E7
A7
keep it clean? (Wal - ly! Wal - ly O'-Ha - ra!)

SONG EXCERPTS

The International

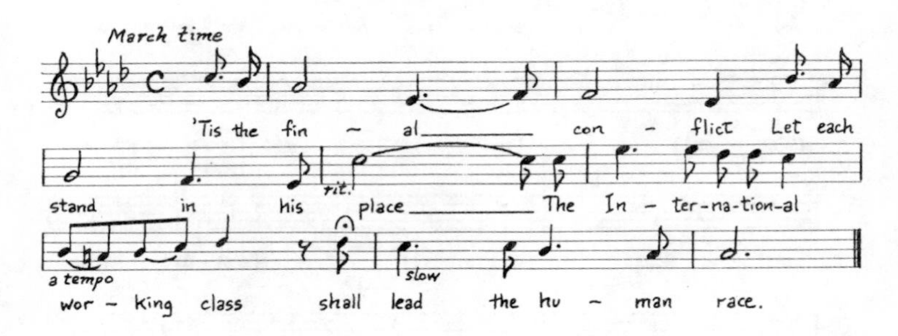

The Fireship

ABOUT LORRAINE HANSBERRY

(*continued from inside front cover*)

about people, Negroes and life." The play, *A Raisin in the Sun*, opened in March 1959—and, as Frank Rich wrote in his *New York Times* review of one of the 25th anniversary productions of that play, it "changed American theatre forever." This was not just because Hansberry, the first black woman produced on Broadway, became at 29 the youngest American, the fifth woman, and the only black dramatist ever to win the Best Play of the Year Award of the New York Drama Critics. *A Raisin in the Sun* marked a turning point because, in James Baldwin's words, "Never before in the entire history of the American theatre had so much of the truth of Black people's lives been seen on the stage."

Published and produced in some thirty languages abroad and in thousands of productions across the U.S., *Raisin* is now firmly established as an American classic. Beyond the universality of its appeal, it also brought into the theatre a new black audience, inspired a generation of black artists, playwrights, performers, and, perhaps most important, on many levels it portended the revolution in consciousness that was to come. For in Rich's words: "With remarkable prescience, she saw history whole: Her play encompasses everything from the rise of black nationalism in the United States and Africa to the advent of black militancy to the specific dimensions of the black women's liberation movement. And she always saw the present and the future in the light of the past."

Lorraine Hansberry lived to see only one other of the several plays to which she devoted the next four years on the stage—*The Sign in Sidney Brustein's Window*, which opened Oct. 15, 1964, while the author was battling cancer. This play confounded the expectations of not a few of the first-night critics, for unlike *Raisin* it did not focus on the black experience but on life in Greenwich Village where she had lived for ten years—and on the need, in an age of increasing alienation, cynicism and despair, for artists, intellectuals, and Americans generally, to take a stand.

"Not unpredictably," Clive Barnes and John Gassner summarized in their introduction to *Brustein* in *Best American Plays*, "the play got what is known in the trade as a 'mixed press.' With few exceptions, Miss Hansberry's play was respectfully, even warmly received. They were the kind of notices that . . . in London's West End might easily have guaranteed a run of anything between six months and a year. But . . . the sad economics of the Broadway theatre are such that when a serious play . . . fails to get almost unanimously rave notices, its fate is virtually sealed."

That did not happen in the case of *Brustein*, however. "The play simply refused to die," Barnes and Gassner continued, as dozens, and then hundreds, of the theatre's leading artists and writers rallied to save it, and ultimately thousands of the public who saw it contributed of their time and money to "keep the Sign in the window." *Sidney Brustein* became "the most talked about play" of the 1964–65 season, and the "remarkable saga" of its 101-day run entered Broadway annals as a "theatrical miracle."*

On January 12, 1965, Lorraine Hansberry died of cancer. She was 34. In her short life she had participated, both as activist and artist, in some of the most momentous events of her time. In her plays, she illuminated the lives and aspirations of ordinary people confronting, in

---

*The full story of these events (and the history of the play itself) is recounted in "The 101 'Final' Performances of *Sidney Brustein*," reprinted from *New York* magazine in the Random House and New American Library editions of the play.

their own way, the fundamental challenges and choices of the age. "Her commitment of spirit . . . her creative literary ability and her profound grasp of the deep social issues confronting the world today," said Martin Luther King Jr., "will remain an inspiration to generations yet unborn."

These words have proved prophetic. *To Be Young, Gifted and Black*, a portrait of Hansberry in her own words, was the longest-running off-Broadway drama of 1969; it has been staged in every state of the Union, recorded, filmed, televised, turned into a popular song by Nina Simone, and the title phrase itself (from her last speech) has entered the language in countless permutations. *Les Blancs* (The Whites), her drama of black/white confrontation in revolutionary Africa, was presented posthumously on Broadway and received the votes of six critics for the Best American Play of 1970. In 1974, the musical *Raisin*, based on *A Raisin in the Sun*, won the Tony Award as Broadway's Best Musical.

Hansberry's published works include *To Be Young, Gifted and Black*, a full-length informal autobiography (not to be confused with the play); *A Raisin in the Sun and The Sign in Sidney Brustein's Window* (a New American Library double-edition); *The Movement: Documentary of a Struggle for Equality* (a photohistory of the civil rights struggle written for the Student Nonviolent Coordinating Committee); and *Lorraine Hansberry: The Collected Last Plays* (Plume Books, New American Library). Highlights from her speeches and interviews can be heard on the Caedmon recording *Lorraine Hansberry Speaks Out: Art and The Black Revolution.* In 1979, *Lorraine Hansberry: Art of Thunder, Vision of Light*, a retrospective assessment by leading writers, critics and playwrights, was published by the quarterly *Freedomways* (New York City).

THE SIGN IN SIDNEY BRUSTEIN'S WINDOW
THROUGH THE YEARS

(*continued from back cover*)

hope to see such perfection in the theatre again. . . . It is a mirror to the life of the human race.''

—Rex Reed, *New York Express*, **1964,** *Playbill*, **1968**

"There is a scene more searing than anything on Broadway. . . . There are other scenes . . . that shine with humor, tremble with feeling and summon up a vision of wisdom and integrity. . . . But the truth must be faced that Miss Hansberry's play lacks . . . cohesion."

—Howard Taubman, *The New York Times*, **1964**

". . . above it all is the stinking triviality of it all . . . extremely poor writing, almost ridiculous plotting and a set of characters that, for sheer implausibility, should win some sort of award."

—Martin Gottfried, *Women's Wear Daily*, **1964**

"It seems incredible that *Sidney Brustein* did not find a large and loving audience in its Broadway run, for here is a play so rich and warm and funny and vital and varied, so beautifully written and wondrously performed, that it is worth a carload of slick little Broadway hits."

—Cecil Smith, *Los Angeles Times*, **1965**

''Even though [*Brustein*] folded at the box office, it lives in Miss Hansberry's vigorous prose. Even in print it is theatre. . . . Her characters leap out of the pages of this paperback book. The dialogue has resonance. The story has momentum . . . remind[ing] us that even a prose play is a form of poetry. It illuminates whole segments of life by the excess of its interior vitality and the breadth of its allusions."

—Brooks Atkinson, *Saturday Review*, **1966**

"*Sidney Brustein* is one of the most important and relevant dramas of our times, more vital today than when it was written. Though it radiates with incisive humor and humanity . . . it challenges the prepackaged attitudes which limit our insights, the *a priori* judgments of right and left which cripple our comprehension. It tricks us by introducing characters that we are too ready to pigeonhole, then shows us that we have been . . . condescending and spiritually anesthetized."

—John Mahoney, *Hollywood Reporter*, **1967**

"One of the two or three best plays to be seen in Miami . . . it is a three-act telescope into a handful of lives . . . in which the playwright and the audience both end up looking through the correct end of the glass for a change."

—Lawrence DeVine, *Miami Herald*, **1967**

"No contemporary playwright, it seems to me, has captured so vividly the fervor and *angst* of certain big-city intellectuals. . . . In this sense *Sidney Brustein*, flawed though it is, is a key play in the history of modern American drama . . . a *tour de force* both in its subtly complex writing, and its philosophical premises."

—Emory Lewis, *Stages: The Fifty-Year Childhood of the American Theatre*, **1969**

"The play was produced a year and a half before white liberal intellectuals were to be confronted by the spectre of black power. *Sign* was a conscious warning. Lorraine Hansberry was speaking to those white intellectuals of her own generation and telling them to prepare for what was to come. . . . she cared enough about her white intellectual counterparts to beg them to prepare to pick up the gauntlet and return to the field. . . . On another level, however, the play is a warning to those of us who are now young as Sidney once was and who will be growing older. . . . Where will we be ten, fifteen years from now, with our books, our records, and our dreams? Where will we be if (or when) the bubble bursts? . . . All of us will, in one way or the other, have to walk the painful road walked by Sidney Brustein and I hope that at the end of it, we can say, as Sidney does, that he is 'a fool . . . who believes. . . .' Her idealism is a kind that we don't have anymore . . . and if that is true, then chaos and barbarism stretch before us into infinity."

—Julius Lester, *Village Voice*, **1970**

"The Arena Stage production is its first major revival; I am glad to report that [*Brustein*] is still a sustaining, nourishing experience. . . . Miss Hansberry is exploring, with compassionate insight, matters that are still just as important as they were in 1964."

—Julius Novick, *The New York Times*, **1971**

"Lorraine Hansberry's stunning view of life and its woes, consequences and possibilities deserves to be seen more than it is, and is so beautifully written that it is hard to bury the potent message under any wrong-doings in the local production. . . . Its authoress died too soon to revise and edit. Nonetheless, her compassionate view of selling out . . . remains one of the modern fortes of the American theatre. —Toy, *Daily Variety*, **1972**

"The strength of Miss Hansberry was in her remarkable ability to write strong theatrical scenes. There are three or four here that in themselves represent some of the best Broadway writing of the last few years. She is a master of the dramatic confrontation—the savage and surprising impact of people upon one another. . . . It is a flawed play, but it has the good red blood of a Broadway success running through it."

—Clive Barnes, *The New York Times*, **1972**

THE SIGN IN SIDNEY BRUSTEIN'S WINDOW *THROUGH THE YEARS*

"One line reflects the major concerns of the late Lorraine Hansberry's drama of belief and responsibility at the Richard Allen Center: 'There are no squares. Believe me, Sidney, everyone is his own hipster.' . . . Everyone stands on his own turf and dares the others to challenge it. The wars are on. However, with Hansberry, these are not just wooden figures up there with toy swords. Each draws our sympathy precisely because everyone *is* right to varying degrees. The playwright skillfully orchestrates our emotions, directing our anger here, our tenderness there, so that we see some of ourselves in all the characters. . . ." —Don Nelsen, *Daily News*, **1980**

". . . and what a revival it is. There isn't a dated line in the show. It is about, among other things, the collapse of the whole liberal-radical moral order into chaos and cynicism . . . a devastating satire on the so-called lifestyles that were the foundations of and gave rise to the Sixties. . . . It is a superpowerful combination of the principal ideas of our times, but with no let-up on emotional and psychological probing of values that so many people have mouthed. In many ways, *Brustein* is her greatest triumph. It turns out that her view of the course of Village liberalism wasn't naive or romantic in the least, but proved prophetic."

—Lionel Mitchell, *N.Y. Amsterdam News*, **1980**

". . . one of the most sensitive and fully developed portraits of a Jew in contemporary drama . . . Hansberry's play affirms faith in the creative energy of the individual whose ultimate loyalty transcends all particular ethnic and ideological designations to reside in '*Man! The human race!*'"

—Ellen Schiff, *From Stereotype to Metaphor: The Jew in Contemporary Drama*, **1982**

LORRAINE HANSBERRY'S

LES BLANCS (THE WHITES)

(DRAMA)

8 men, 3 women, extras (incl. child)—Interior and exterior unit set

Hansberry's last major drama, voted by five critics Best American Play of 1970, prophetically confronts the hope and tragedy of modern Africa in revolution. The setting is an African village and a white Christian mission in a colony about to explode. The time is now, in that hour of reckoning when no one—the guilty and innocent alike—can evade the imperatives of black African liberation. Tshembe Matoseh, son of a chief, educated at the mission and in England, has come home to bury his father. He finds his younger brother has become an alcoholic, his older brother a priest—and a traitor to his people. Foreswearing politics, wanting only to return to his wife and child in England, he finds himself drawn irrevocably into the conflict. The characters include the matriarch of the mission, one of Hansberry's most penetrating female portraits; the homosexual surgeon who has come to serve humanity in a cause he now questions; a Scandinavian woman doctor who supports the old order; the "faithful" house servant, an insurgent leader; the commander of the District; and a liberal American journalist in caustic interaction with whom, the arguments of all are honed. In the crucial decisions each makes, the crisis of the modern world is mirrored.

"An incredibly moving experience . . . towering, magnificent. . . . a work ready to stand without apology alongside the completed work of our best craftsmen."—*NY Times*. "Possessed of the unrelenting power, breadth of vision and masterly technique that only a very few playwrights are capable of in any one generation. The play is a collision course between the races and Ms. Hansberry's plotting of it is wise, sure, ironic, clear-eyed, and electrifying in the drive and finality of its tragedy."—*Detroit News*. "The best American play this season! What a striking, forceful and essentially fair-minded playwright Lorraine Hansberry was!"—*NY Post*.

RAISIN

(THE MUSICAL)

Based on A RAISIN IN THE SUN

8 men, 6 women, 1 child, extras—Interior and exterior unit set

Based on Lorraine Hansberry's classic drama of a Black family's attempt to attain the American Dream. Book by Robert Nemiroff and Charlotte Zaltzberg. Music by Judd Woldin. Lyrics by Robert Brittan. Winner of both Tony and Grammy Awards as Broadway's Best Musical, *Raisin* draws upon the best dialogue and most dramatic moments in the original play to tell the same story: of a son's desperate ambition for "success" as America defines it; of his wife's and mother's dream of buying a home in a neighborhood where the family can find a little "sunlight" and the children a better chance at survival; of his independent-minded younger sister with a dream of her own; and of the heartbreak and racial conflict they encounter, the mother's heroic struggle to hold them together, and the power of love and family bonds. Utilizing gospel, jazz, blues, African, and traditional musical comedy idioms to heighten and underscore the universal dimensions of this story, the musical spills out of the Youngers' ghetto flat into the streets, bars, churches and workaday worlds of Southside Chicago to explode in song and dance, drama and comedy. Like the original, it affirms Hansberry's prophetic themes of Afro-American identity, beauty, pride, and the imperatives of liberation. At the deepest level, it is a celebration of life—of the joy and beauty of a family coming into their own, standing up for themselves and their heritage as people, as Blacks, as men and women.

"Pure magic . . . dazzling! Tremendous! . . . *Raisin* warms the heart and touches the soul. A musical delight . . . with a human dimension that takes the measurement of man."—*NY Times*. "A musical blockbuster! One of the happiest of all American musicals ever."—*Boston Herald American*. "A tidal wave of soul!"—*Ebony Magazine*. "A musical to treasure forever."—*Washington Post*.